# Punch & Pie

## A SHORT STORY ANTHOLOGY

edited by
Felizon Vidad and Todd Taylor

GORSKY PRESS
LOS ANGELES • CALIFORNIA
2003

# Punch & Pie



Earlier versions of "The New Kid Has an Old Bicycle" by Wred Fright have appeared in *A Cup Of Fiction #2* and *drinkdrankdrunk #1*. An earlier version of "A Terrible Thing in a Place like This" by Jim Ruland appeared in *Fictionline*. "Marauders" by Jerry Gabriel originally appeared in *Writers' Forum*. All other stories are previously unpublished. 

***Special thanks to Sean Carswell for helping to select the authors in this collection, for designing the cover, and for everything else.***

The cover photo and all the interior photos were taken by Dan Monick. Thanks Lil' Hairy.

ISBN 0-966-8185-6-3

**Gorsky Press**
**PO Box 42024**
**LA, CA 90042**
**www.gorskypress.com**

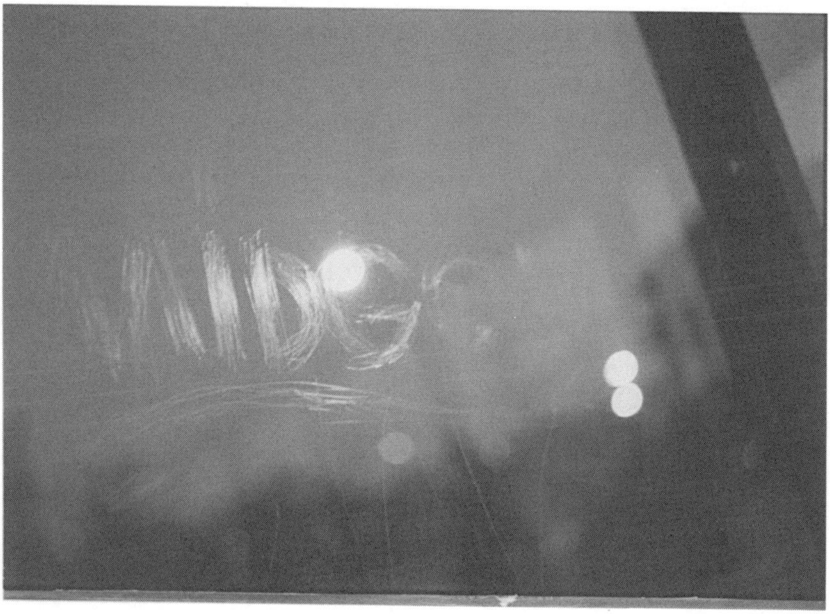

# TABLE OF CONTENTS

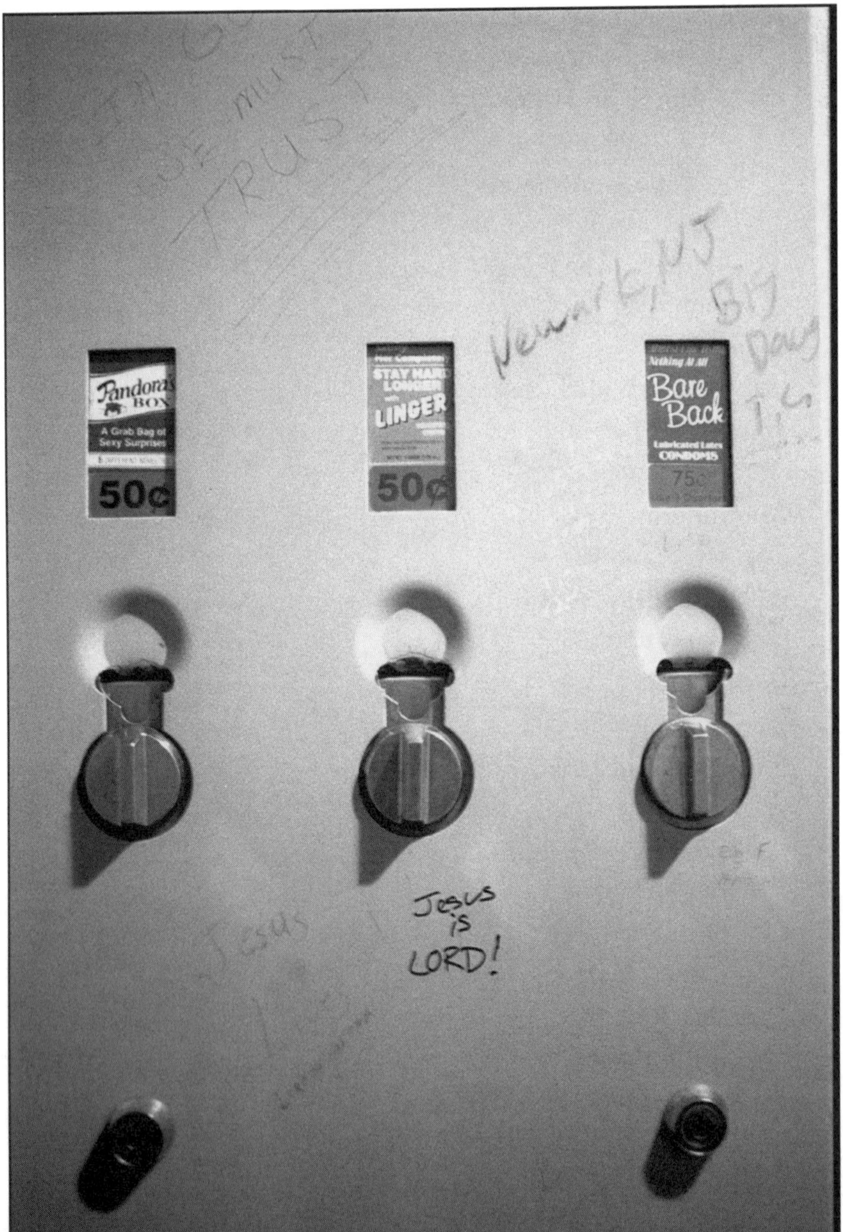
WE MUST
TRUST
Newark, NJ
Pandora's
BOX
A Grab Bag of
Sexy Surprises
50¢
STAY HARD
LONGER
with
LINGER
50¢
Nothing At All
Bare
Back
Lubricated Latex
CONDOMS
75¢
Jesus
is
LORD!

# Diddy's Cardinal Rule of Driving

Bradley Williams

The wedding had been an outdoor affair, with a reception that lead from a club where some bands had played, to back across the Mobile Bay bridge, and ending up at what could have been a third-world Ramada Inn. The Ramada, surrounded by overgrown weeds and other various unattended greenery, sat on a small outlet of land only a few feet above the water line. You could see the sign for about a mile until you finally got to the hotel. The *R* was burnt out so what it said was *amada*. Yes, we had spent the night in the Amada, drinking heavily and hitting on the bridesmaids. But that was last night. This morning we had gotten up and gone with a few other people to a seafood restaurant to get some shrimp and oysters. The food had been salted to hell and back, and being that we were hung over didn't help. But I was back home in Alabama, after months in Los Angeles, and now me and Diddy were without an air conditioner and heading north on I-65.

With sunglasses on and the windows rolled down, we were feeling cool in the heat. My hair was getting blown into tangles, but Diddy didn't have to worry about that because Diddy was bald. It's not that he shaves his head, but that it won't grow there. Diddy was bitching about how he's been getting sick to his stomach for the past few miles. Diddy don't like to stop while he's driving. He'd rather piss in a bottle than pull over.

"Damned it, Diddy, we can't even get out of Mobile before you get sick," I said, just to fuck with him.

"Kiss my ass, pecker-lip. Diddy's got to hit a service station. We're getting off at the next one."

A few miles up the road, we got off I-65 and stopped at a Chevron. Diddy was out of the car running. I walked in behind him as the service station attendant was pointing the way to the bathroom.

I was flat broke, which is nothing out of the ordinary, except that this time I was broke because, leaving the wedding, I was slightly intoxicated and had gotten some money out of an ATM machine, but I left the card in the machine and didn't realize it till the following day. I didn't need anything anyway, but it was too hot to go sit in the car so I busied myself by studying a map of the waterways and tributaries of the Mobile Bay.

The bay is a lot more complex than I had thought. I was trying to find the Amada amongst the natural flowing, jagged shore lines and the squared off, flat manmade docks and canals. I decided that one day I'd own a boat and I'd come down here and explore the entire bay. But before I could do that, I'd have to acquire a boat. Which meant I had to have money. You don't get boats by losing your ATM cards because you're drunk coming from a wedding. But that's just how it goes sometimes.

Diddy had been in the bathroom for a while and I was starting to wonder if he was alive in there. I waited. Two large ladies came in the front door with a little girl. They went straight for the women's room. I wished Diddy would hurry up. I was dirty and it felt like everyone was staring at me. You're just being paranoid, I thought. About that time Diddy came out of the bathroom strutting.

"You all right?" I asked.

"Shuew... I don't know," Diddy said as he whipped some sweat from his brow and a cringe crept upon his face, "I got to go back."

"Damn it, Diddy, hurry up," I said as he made his way back to the bathroom.

When Diddy closed the door to the bathroom, I caught a whiff of the effervescent crap he'd been laying down in that room. Damn, it was strong. I went back to studying the maps. I still couldn't find the damned Amada.

The women's bathroom door creaked open and I could hear the ladies talking as they stepped out of the room and smelled the present Diddy had left them.

"Damn, Vanessa, is that you smells like that?" said the biggest lady.

"No. It's not me," said the little girl.

"Lord, girl, I hope that's not you. Oh damn!" said the other lady.

"Y'all get y'all's drinks and let's go before Vanessa gets sick," the biggest lady said.

"I ain't sick!"

They got their stuff, paid, and left. Diddy came back out of the bathroom.

"You ready, boy?" Diddy asked.

"Hell, you're making fans out here," I said.

"What in the hell are you talking about, boy?"

"You don't smell that?" I said. "People are trying to stand in here 'cause it's too hot to stand outside, and you are back in there stinking it all up."

Diddy goes, "You can smell it?"

"Hell yeah, you can smell it!" I said. "Now let's get out of here before someone tries to ask you for an autograph or arrest you."

Earlier that morning I'd gotten in touch with a friend of mine, and he'd invited us over for the night. "We'll get drunk and play croquet," he said. "The stinking Brits hate American croquet because we get drunk when we play." I don't know why he had to bring Britain into it, but it sounded like fun. I told him we'd be there.

We were back on I-65 northbound, and it was still hot as hell. Me and Diddy started talking. We talked about girls. He told me about the troubles and likes of his girls, and I shared some fucked-up tales of my own. There is nothing like talking about women to make a long, hot drive go by a little easier. Except, that is, if there had been girls in the car with us, but we had failed at that the night before. Either we weren't smooth enough, or we scared the cute little southern flowers.

"I can't believe you didn't kiss Sarah last night," said Diddy.

"Fuck off about that," I told him. "I tried and she didn't want anything to do with me."

"Yeah, she shuts them all down," he said, "and the ones she likes are all fucked up."

"How do you mean?" I asked.

"I don't know; they're all fucking stupid," he said.

"What do you mean? Like what do they do?" I asked.

"Hell, it don't matter. Ain't none of them getting anything off her anyway," he said.

"Really?"

"Yeah, she don't put out."

"Damn," I said. "She's a cutie."

"She hung out with Carl for six months and they fucked maybe twice," Diddy told me.

"How the hell do you know that?"

"From Lisa," he said.

Damn, I thought, glad I'm not Carl.

"Did I tell you about this guy I work with?" Diddy started. "His girlfriend showed us her tits the other night." And he leaned back as pride swept across his face.

We rode on—sunglasses, wind, and talking about women.

It was smooth like that until Diddy broke the stream with, "You like chicken gizzards?"

"Hell no!" I said. "I don't eat that shit."

"Come on boy, they're good," he said. "Tastes just like chicken."

"I ate them once and they're fucking nasty," I replied.

"Hell, keep an eye out. We're going to get some." Diddy was excited by just the thought of gizzards.

We picked the conversation back up somewhere around the sounds my fourth girlfriend would make when she came, and time passed right on by as we went up I-65. For a while we weren't noticing places to get gizzards until we had already passed them. Diddy kept count by cussing. Then we saw a Stuckey's. Diddy exited. Diddy excited.

There was one thing about Stuckey's that Diddy, in his gizzard fever, wasn't aware of, and that was Stuckey's doesn't sell fried chicken, and most likely they don't have gizzards. When Diddy read the menu and discovered this, it pissed him off to high heaven. Not only did they not have any gizzards, but Diddy had had trouble finding a parking spot, and he had exited the interstate and that was a waste of time, and damn it, Diddy didn't like to waste time when he was driving.

We were back heading north again when I saw a billboard. I said, "Diddy, there's a KFC up ahead."

"They got gizzards?"

"They're KFC; I think that they would."

We made the exit and pulled into the KFC drive-thru.

"KFC. Hold."

"That's no damn way to talk," Diddy said. "You'd think them stupid sons of bitches could at least say *welcome* and *please*. Fuck no, they won't!" he said. Then, while he was looking for gizzards on the menu he mocked, "Fucking *KFC*, *hold*," and, in a matter of seconds, Diddy was sent into a rage. "What kind of fucking drive-thru is this?" he said as he read the menu. "They don't have no fucking gizzards!"

"What?" I read the menu. "Shit, I guess they don't," I said. "We'll just have to look for a good and greasy truck stop."

"Godfuckndamnit!" Diddy said as he hit the steering wheel. "I'm in the heart of Alabama, and I can't find any goddamned gizzards! Fuck!"

We pulled out of the KFC drive-thru, went about twenty yards, and pulled into a Shell service station. As we opened the door to go in, we saw the glass-fronted, silver-framed, hot food line, and a big white girl using tongs to throw fried chicken legs in one of the warmer's steel baskets.

"I don't fucking believe it," Diddy announced. "Please tell me y'all have got gizzards?"

The big girl threw the last chicken leg in the basket, turned, and tossed the basket on a metal pan by the fryer. She looked at Diddy. She didn't look happy—like something was eating at her. "Gizzards?" she asked. "Why don't you go to KFC and get your gizzards?"

"We're just there and they ain't got none," I said.

"Yeah, they don't say nothing about them on the menu," said Diddy.

The big girl looked over to the man behind the register and drew her eyebrows together. It was a look that said she was searching for something, maybe approval, or maybe she was looking to draw his attention towards me and Diddy.

"You got to ask for them," she said. "They ain't on no menu."

"Ask for them?" Diddy said.

"Yeah," said the big girl. "Just like Captain D's and stuffed crab. It ain't on the menu, but if you ask for them, they got them."

Diddy agreed. "Captian D's does have stuffed crab."

I wasn't paying this any more attention. I figured we'd be out of the store in a minute and heading back over to the KFC so Diddy could ask for his gizzards which aren't on the menu, but, as I imagined, must be kept in a clear plastic bag, covered with frost, inside an old, smashed up box, one that probably has holes in it from where when someone gets pissed off, they go in the cooler to get away from the heat of the fryers, and shut the thick, insulated door, and scream, and punch holes in the box of frozen gizzards that no one orders, because, if they don't know to ask for them, then they don't know they have them.

It was then that I noticed the lighters.

I paused. Diddy was excited and making his way out the door when I called him back. "Diddy," I said, "get over here and tell me what the fuck this is."

"What what is?" asked the big girl.

I ignored her. "Diddy, get your ass back here and look at this," I repeated.

"What the hell is it?" he said. "I want my gizzards, boy."

"Look at this," I said and pointed to the lighters on the counter. The big girl and the man behind the counter looked at each other with equal skepticism then leaned forward.

"What?" Diddy said and leaned in for a closer look. "What the fuck is that?"

"I don't fucking know," I replied.

Of course it was a lighter. It was just one of the many variations of the novelty lighters that you can see inside any gas station across America. But what made these any different? They weren't any of the variations of blow torch lighters that people call crack lighters. No, these were normal lighters. With one exception. It was the artwork on the lighter that caught my attention. At first I thought what I had seen was an old *Star Wars* lighter. A fuzzy, miniature reprint of a painting of Luke Skywalker in his white robe that he wore in the first movie. It made sense to me. Maybe someone was trying to cash in off the *Star Wars* hype. But something was strange about it. It wasn't Luke. Unless Luke had an afro I wasn't aware of. No. The picture on the lighter was of a black man with an afro, wearing a white robe and standing in front of… what looked like a backdrop of space, but with orange triangles, blue squares, and green circles in the place of where you might expect to see planets. That was strange, but not as strange as the next lighter.

On the second lighter was a bat. No big deal. Except riding on the bat was a shirtless man who resembled He-Man, carrying a sword, raised in the air above his head. This lighter had the same miniature, hand-painted look as the first one. It was fuzzy and the detail was not that great. But in the scope of novelty lighters, it stood out.

And so I asked the man behind the counter, "What is the deal with these lighters?"

"Which ones?" he asked.

"These here with the paintings on them," I said.

He leaned forward. "Well," he said, "these on the top are fifty cents 'cause they are small. The middle ones here are a dollar, and them with the picture are a dollar twenty-five… 'cause they got a picture, I suppose." He cocked his eyebrows and gave me a questioning look.

"I figured that," I said, "but why have they got a bat and a guy with a sword riding it?"

"Cause it's a dollar twenty-five," he said. "I guess they charge more for the picture."

I looked at him.

"Leave him the hell alone," said Diddy.

"But why the hell they got a…"

"You know why," said Diddy. "It's to make you stop and look at that ugly-ass painting and then spend that last dollar you got on some damned stupid lighter." Diddy paused then added, "Hell, you ain't even got a dollar. Let's get down there and get some gizzards, boy!"

I turned to the man behind the counter and the big girl and said thank you and good bye. The old man waved and the big girl gave me a look that said go to hell. I didn't care about the look. She wasn't happy about something and I didn't know what.

Diddy got his gizzards and we were back on the highway heading north.

Diddy goes, "Try one of these gizzards."

I said, "Hell no, I ain't eating that shit."

"They damned good, boy," said Diddy and dipped one of the fried gizzards in the ranch dressing that came with them. "You've been out of the South too long if you ain't eatn' gizzards."

"I ate them one time from the Conoco by Little Irelands, in Auburn. They were cold and gritty. I didn't like that shit."

"Fine. You're a pussy. You done turned into a Califag," he said. "Just try one. If you don't like it, spit it out the window. It ain't going to kill you."

I grabbed the damned gizzard, dipped it in the ranch dressing, and popped it in my mouth. I chewed it once, then swallowed. Diddy handed me the box and I ate another. I chewed this one to a fine pulp. Diddy could kiss my ass.

I don't eat many internal organs, unless you consider pig skin an organ; other than that, gizzards are the only organs I'd ever ate. There's something about eating organs, that, if you're not used to them, they feel dirty. But it's a welcome dirty—one that fits in with the heat, and the thought of women—many of whom I'm sure would not be impressed with the telling of this story, but as a Los Angeles bum, known by the name Running Backwards Man, once said to me on the Sunset Strip while jogging in place and wearing a yellow rope that held up his blue shorts, "Don't talk about women first. First comes matters of the soul." I looked over at Diddy. He wasn't looking good. Like maybe he was holding his stomach in his mouth.

"You alright, fuck nut?" I asked.

"I'm going to have to pull over again," he said, which was followed by his muffled frustration at once again having to break the Diddy Cardinal rule of driving: piss in a bottle 'cause we ain't stopping. "Fucking goddamned it!" he screamed, then pounded his fist on the steering wheel as he exited a fourth time, and not even halfway to our rendezvous with American-style, drunken croquet.

Diddy parked in the shade, so I decided this time I would stay in the car. I thought about the lighters. I didn't know what the point of them was. I was obsessing. All things must have a point, I thought. Could Diddy have been right? Was the lighter meant to be ridiculous just to grab my attention? For that to work, I would have to assume that what I found strange must also be considered strange by others, and since I don't get a newsletter from the National Strange Stuff Club informing me, and I suppose others, on what is strange, I can't assume that. Or I would have to assume that the people who made those lighters had banked on other people in remote areas of Alabama sharing in their humor. Was it humor? Was it some kind of joke? What kind of individual would paint a shirtless He-Man-type character brandishing a sword while flying through the night skies on the back of a bat? Was it some sort of outcast, a separated individual who came up with it? A high school D & D player who never made it with the rest of the world and had somehow managed to find a niche for his or her art on the faces of lighters? I wanted to know.

Diddy was back.

"You doing better?" I asked.

"Son, your Diddy thought he wasn't going to make it," he said.

I thought… I hesitated… Then I asked, "Diddy, what do think was really up with those lighters?"

"You still thinking about them fucking lighters?" Diddy said. "You're a dumbass! I forgot about that shit soon as we got in the car."

"Yeah, but you were eating your fucking gizzards."

"You ate some too."

"But that don't mean… ah, fuck it," I said. "I just thought the lighters were fucked up. There's no telling what they meant. Just weird."

"To hell with it. Look back in the back and give me one of them Buschs."

"They're hot."

"I know. That's why I got a cup of ice."

"You got a cup of ice for your beer? Can't you wait till we get to where we're going? There'll be croquet and cold beer."

"How hot are they?"

"They're fucking scorching. You don't need no damned beer."

"Ah, fuck!"

Diddy got back on the road.

"You think we can try and not stop before we get there?" I said.

"Yeah, I think I can make it."

We rode on down the road. Then I asked, "So what was your last lady like?"

Diddy looked out the window at the passing pine trees. The windows down, the air boiling.

"Well," he started, "she shaved everything…"

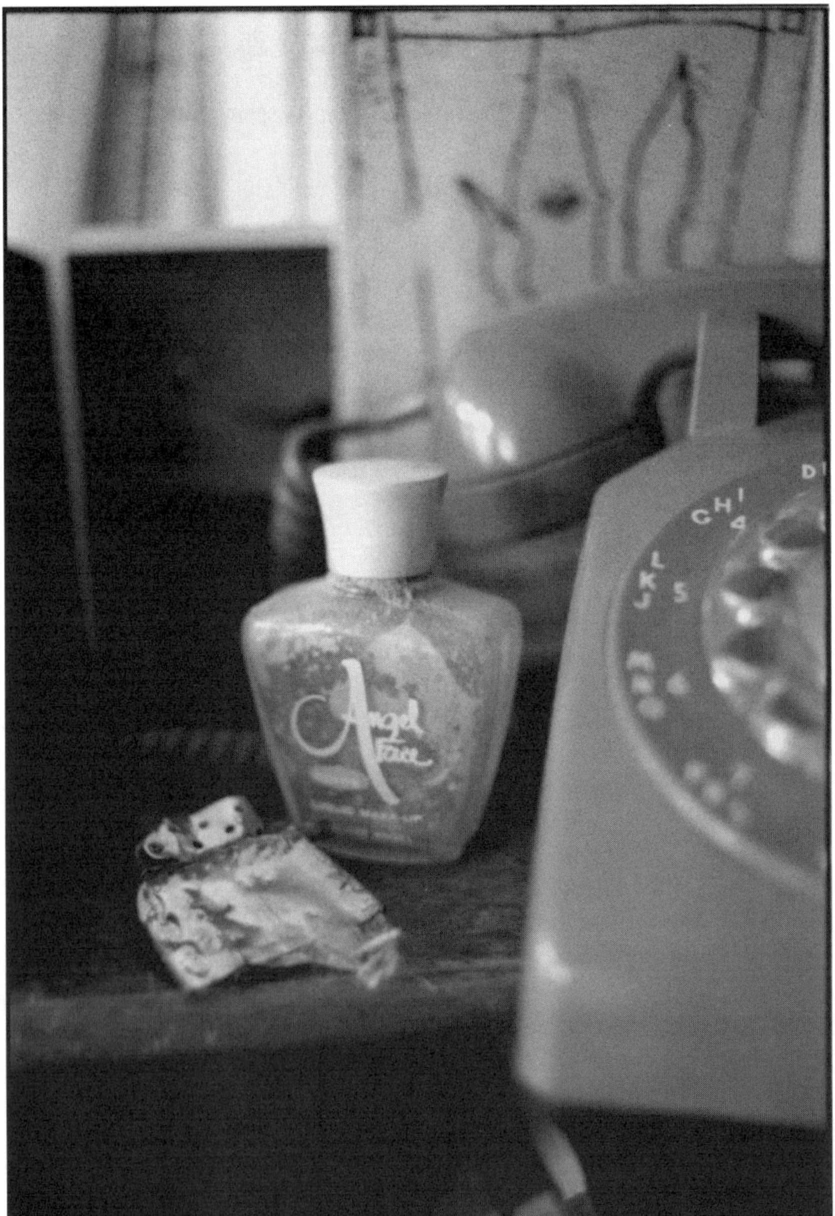
Angel Face
GHI 4
JKL 5

# Little Angels in Water

Ayn Imperato

Manna's face hung completely still, her mouth fallen into a grim mask as she plod down Larkin Street towards the south side of town. Her half-closed eyes were portholes to the sky, clear blue, motionless. The Xanax made it like this. Made thoughts more like dreams, bending up through the San Francisco sky forever. She mixed it with other drugs in slim brown bottles. Drugs with names as long and jointed as centipedes, with lots of x's and y's. Her thoughts crowded together and slipped away like insects swarming and dissipating into the immense city skyline.

She shuffled down the pee-scented sidewalk towards the subway in a fucked-up red dress. A strappy dress with stains and holes, though once it had been nice. A flurry of catcalls rang out as she pulled the hem down absentmindedly, futilely yanking the red fabric down over another inch of exposed thigh.

Manna watched the life around her in a series of images. Her world flipped past like frames in a film, slowed down to reveal each milky, celluloid square. People passed by her in a train of heavy shapes, each moment a new lumbering car—disjointed city parts, sounds flashing, alcoholics lying in the street.

She took the K car, outbound. On the train she simply sat, staring out at the dark space outside the window, watching the tunnel rush by in a black wash of speed. It was like her thoughts, coming and going without a chance to grab hold. She ran her fingers vaguely across the top of her head. Her choppy blond hair stuck out and was dirty. Lines crept from the corners of her eyes. A man in a business suit sitting across from her stared openly.

"It's not going to Brunswick," a woman standing in the aisle said to no one. She was wearing a red knit cap with the ears cut out. The other passengers glanced at her and looked away. The lights flickered.

"I'll be here all night," the red-capped woman stated. She stared at the gum-studded floor.

As Manna stood to leave, the lights flashed off and on. In the flickering moment, the man across from her glanced down at the hem of her skirt. The lights shuddered off again. She thought of the man forced to stare down at darkness. She stepped off before they snapped back on.

The photographer's house was a blue squat building, one level with a long rectangular front window. She rang the bell. A tall, wide man opened the door. "I'm George," he said. His face was hideously pockmarked. "You must be Mantra." She stared blankly through him. There was a silent, lengthy pause. Around them civilizations rose and fell.

"Okay, well, come in."

"Manna," she said, too late. He had turned and begun to walk down the long hallway. His pant legs were wide and hung straight down to the floor over the tops of his shoes, covering them. As he walked, his legs moved like fat, swishy strips.

"Gumby," she mumbled, with a slight grin.

"What?" He stopped and turned around.

"Hungry," she stated. She looked at him holding a vague grin, staring off into her head, into frames of polluted sky.

"I don't have any food," he said, clipped. "I can get you a drink if you want—"

"No," she said, a bit too fast. Drinks didn't work well with the drugs.

He led her into a spacious living room with ceramic figurines littered everywhere, on shelves, end tables. There seemed to be a lobster theme. A large green ceramic crustacean hung from the back wall, claws out, pinching the sky.

He stood in the center of the room and looked at her chest. "I thought you were younger. You said you were younger." He began pinching his thumb and forefinger together in rapid succession.

"I'm twenty." She paused. "Eight." Even that, they both knew, was a lie. He grimaced.

"Sign this," he announced brusquely, pointing to a release form on the glass coffee table. She glanced at the paper. There was a round buoy cork parked next to it over a net that swarmed under the glass tabletop.

Manna gazed out through the oblong window. It was overcast outside, a gray muted haze around the pastel Victorian homes. She was alarmed as a mousy woman in a fuchsia jogging suit strolled past the window at a decent clip.

"Three hundred, right?" she asked.

George grunted, "Uh huh." Manna picked up the pen and signed.

She dumped her bag on the table and showed him what she had brought—a ragged black lace bra and thong, a red teddy circa '70s, a pair of scuffed crimson platform heels. George looked at the lacy heap and frowned.

"I want this to look *real*," he emphasized, "like you're a school girl just, you know, hanging out at home." He held out a pair of white high-waisted cotton briefs. "Will you put these on?" She reached her limp hand forward, in slow motion, and he draped the briefs over her curved hand like hanging them on a hook.

After she changed, she plod out of the bathroom in bare feet. The briefs were small and the elastic dug into her waist creating a ridge of flab. Her eyelids hung at half-mast. He had pulled the couch out into a bed covered with little satin pillows over a ridiculous flower print sheet. "Okay, now just sit up there and have FUN!"

She lay there, propped up on the pillows in the cotton briefs, barefoot. In pigtails. The skin around her eyes was cracked and wrinkled in the glaring light. The photographer scuttled around her, bending and weaving. "Oh, that's it. That's NICE! Now hold your breasts! Be nice to them. *Nice* breasts, *nice* breasts. Look into the camera, now, smile!"

She stared vacantly into the milky lens, watched the black shutter close and separate again.

"Now, get up on your knees and start pulling the panties down."

She rose up and yanked on the waistband.

"Not too fast! Just a little. We want to tease. *Tease*! Come on, flirt with me!" He was whipped into a frenzy, snapping and scuttling. To Manna his small blue eyes looked wild in that crazy pockmarked head. Two eyes peeking out of a red misshapen moon.

"Now turn around. Let's see that great rear!"

She turned and slipped the briefs down slowly over her fairly wide ass. "Holy cantaloupes!" he shouted. Then snapped a few butt shots.

She pulled the briefs off and lay back on the pillows. She looked past the photographer, past the hundred lobster figurines into the space in her mind. For a moment she became a small girl, watching the fish tanks in the basement of Woolworth's department store. She liked to look at them. Inside the tanks was another world, rippling, dreamy, with shiny silver fish that glided like little angels in water. Like grace.

As she watched the fish, a man walked up beside her wearing stained, rotting jeans. Also to watch. After a minute of watching, he tore a plastic bag from the roll above them and started opening the lids of the tanks. He caught the fish one by one in a tiny green net and put them in the plastic bag without any water. When he had a heap of colorful fish inside, flipping gently, he folded the plastic bag up into a roll, stuffed it into his back jeans pocket and exited the store.

"All right, let's spread 'em," George laughed. He snapped a few shots. He walked over and picked up a Snoopy doll from the end table. "Hold this."

"I don't want to, George."

"Oh, come on. It'll be fine." He thrust the doll at her. Between her knees the white animal appeared—a large and shapeless mass. *Three hundred dollars. Three hundred dollars.*

Manna lay back, the white fur doll clutched in her fingers, crushed against her left breast. *I'm 38 years old holding a Snoopy doll,* she thought. Through the frame of her open legs she saw the photographer circling around this body she did not, at this moment, own or belong in. It was as though she was floating above, looking down at someone else lying there. Someone else's hand closed around the obscene plush toy.

"Now put these on." He handed her a pair of pink slippers. The thin terry cloth kind that a grandma might wear, with flat plastic soles to flap across the kitchen floor. "These look natural."

*On an eighty-year-old*, she thought, sliding them on. She raised one slippered foot slowly. The Xanax was really kicking in. The photographer stopped and stood straight up. He examined her for a moment, his mouth a slit.

"Can't you look more—" he paused, regarding her limp, raised foot, "alive?"

She looked at the pink foot, floating in the lobster room. She smiled. For the first time all day it broke across her face. She started to laugh, uncontrollably. Impossibly loud and long.

Her eyes were closed, sealed shut with the force of the laughing. It broke inside her and refused to let up, shaking her body with hysteria. She opened her eyes after what must have been several minutes to find George in a panic, pacing around on the tan carpet, his fingers pinching the air.

Suddenly it was gone. The laugh had slipped away. She could barely even remember the laugh, though knew somewhere inside that it had been a very bad thing to do.

"What is wrong with you?" he asked. "What *was* that?"

"You said," she murmured, looking at the stuffed fish on the wall, "you wanted me alive."

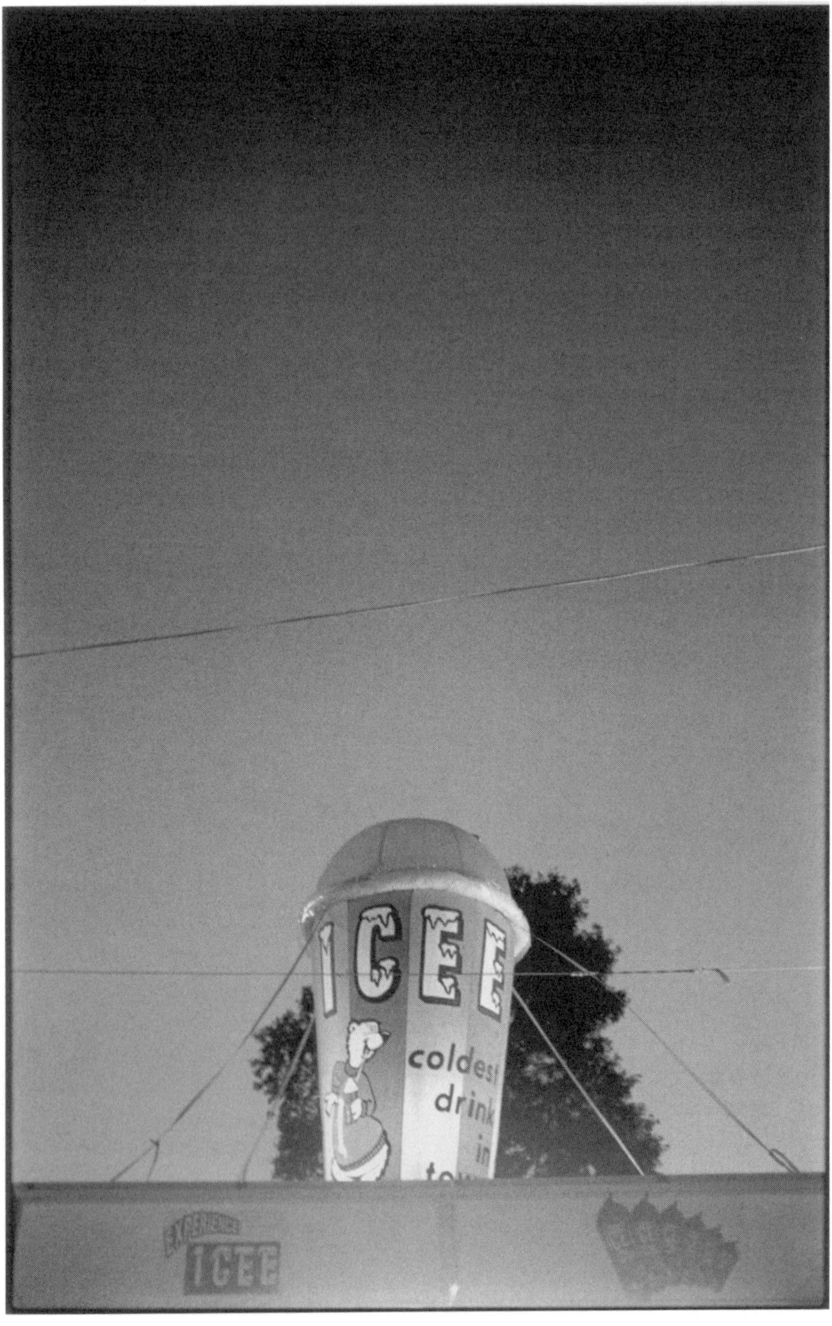
ICEE
coldest
drink
in
ICEE

# A Foregone Contusion

Todd Taylor

It was a vicious hit. The lawnmower was fifteen feet off the ground when it mated with the redwood's trunk. Instead of rounding the corner, Marvin had skittered into a pile of rocks which acted nicely as a launch ramp. It was an accidental flight. Marvin had been meaning to spread the pile out into his dirt driveway so it wouldn't muddy up in the spring.

Neither man could have foreseen the exact situation before it unraveled. They remained very focused, if not a little more than drunk, when the lawnmower was mid-air. It had been a mellow Sunday afternoon up 'til then. A beer bottle rolling under the brake pedal pulled the duo into an unexpected situation.

Otis was a precision drunk driver and while in flight, his instincts reigned. Time went slowly, like single frames clacking through a View Master, one distinct scene at a time. He held onto the cowboy knob on the steering wheel, attempting to keep the front wheels as straight as possible. The situation would be worse if he rolled the lawnmower when it landed. He methodically placed his coolied beer back into the holder near the choke and waited for the impact. He thought he'd eased his foot off the accelerator but was mistaken. Good thing they'd rigged up a seatbelt. It was one of those fancy NASCAR jobbies, too. It held Otis tightly as the blade began skinning some bark.

The two men had rebuilt the lawnmower from the ground up, piece by piece, except for the skin of its chassis, which they crudely painted a turtle with long flames leaping out of its butt. They wanted to make the world's fastest lawnmower.

Marvin's wife had died ten years before. He missed her greatly. She had been an avid, particular gardener with a green fist. Otis's wife wanted a large lawn, which she'd received, and he mowed the best he could to look like a major league baseball outfield with fancy cross hatches. Both of their wives had been in their town's Chamber of Commerce, and as they were wont to do, volunteered their husbands into civic duty. When Marvin and Otis first met, they were wearing red, white, and blue ribbons in their hats and began to learn to carouse their rideable lawnmowers around without ramming into one another. They were part of Toro! Toro! Toro!, the Boulder Precision Lawnmower Drill Team. They perfected complex, synchronized swimming-type flutterings with ten other men for a decade's worth of Fourth of July parades. They felt fruity. They felt like tools. They loved their wives dearly. They, secretly, got very drunk before each outing. They began to think that their rideable lawnmowers had vast, untapped possibility. They wanted speed. They wanted danger. They continued to mow their respective lawns.

By day, Marvin was a nuclear physicist. By weekend and evening, he owned a garage full of tools he knew how to use and machines that could make any metal part he could imagine, which was a considerable asset.

Going back and forth, over the years, they'd weighed the plusses and minuses of removing the lawnmower blade.

"Conceptually," Otis had surmised, "the blade's the only thing that retains the vehicle's 'lawnmowerness.' Otherwise, you're running into go-cart territory." As any niche market is susceptible to rivalry, these two men hated go-carts with a deep-seated passion, just by the fact that they had to deal with the glory-hogging, burn-victim-embracing Shriner fucks during the parades.

Marvin had several framed 8 x 10s of his dead wife in the house. On an adjacent wall, there were two smaller snapshots of his lawnmower from different angles.

Marvin agreed with Otis's theoretics about "lawnmowerness." Yet, more importantly, he needed it to cut his grass, and it was the only fully operational mower he had. Well, up until it hit the tree.

Otis, right before impact, braced himself. Then he yelled to the tree, somewhat cryptically, "I'm going to decimate you to the color of fuck!" How did Marvin know his Gallagher-looking friend with a strawberry blonde mustache wasn't yelling at him? Otis was pointing directly at the tree, calling it out like they were on a grade school playground.

It was an incredible landing. Otis's secondary luck was phenomenal. Oh, the lawnmower was gonna get fucked up, but the forty-three-year-old man didn't impact the tree's trunk right off the bat. No, he skimmed on a long and wide branch, dismembering a random limb or two growing off of it. Lucky? The branch steadied the pitch and yaw of the mower, slowing Otis down ever so slightly, so it was as clean a hit as he'd hoped. Toothpick-sized slivers of redwood showered down.

Then there was the sound of technology getting cracked up against some heavy wood.

The mower's blade dislocated with a gigantic ptwang sound and thwomped towards the ground like a shot-down helicopter. The blade stuck deep into the rich soil, like a medieval sword, about three feet to Marvin's left. Marvin was wearing a helmet also, but that blade would have cut him clean in two. The danger of their hobby didn't escape him as he looked up through goggled eyes, hoping the damage to both his friend and his favorite riding companion was superficial.

It was time for reflection, not panic. The throttle remained open. The engine pipped and panged loudly. The customized exhaust pipe—that looked like a chrome anaconda swallowing a miniature pig—poking out the back, shot out copious amounts of barely white smoke, signs that the engine was still running fine but the accelerator was still being goosed.

Perhaps not wise nor prudent, they were logical men. If the two hadn't just finished their second twelve-pack of Lucky Lagers while fine tuning and testing out the new titanium clutch plates for the first time, the proceedings possibly wouldn't have gone so awry. Agreed. But right then they needed solutions, not a moral middle finger.

"Otis," Marvin yelled, "take your foot off the accelerator!" Marvin put down his beer so he could wave his arms wildly, like he was signaling a rescue airplane. This caught Otis's attention.

Marvin made exaggerated motions, pretending to take his foot off the accelerator. He felt like a mime, and it was a dirty feeling since he really hated mimes and dismissed miming culture as a grave misappropriation of human energy.

Otis shook his head. He didn't understand. The engine roared. Deep in the cockles of that amazing little engine was Marvin's hidden universe. With tiny pieces of metal and their association with one another, he could reconstruct atoms—ones he could see—which made that little maniac of a machine purr. Imagine how a cardiovascular surgeon would feel sewing the heart of a lion into a chihuahua, but far less sinister and without the creepy soundtrack of a mad scientist. His engine was so real. He could feel it vibrate and give off heat when it was bolted to his workbench, tested, and refined over the past eight years. With each turn of its tiny crank, the memory of his wife's death stabbed his heart less and less.

Amazingly, in the limber yoga of branches and fate, the lawnmower appeared firmly couched onto the tree's trunk. Otis, although dazed, regained his bearings and saw his good friend, in shorts, although it was fall, making some odd motions with his foot. Otis looked down to his own, saw it was depressing the accelerator, and figured that was why there was such a tremendous din. Thusly, he removed his foot. The lawnmower's engine decelerated to a harmonious idle. His mouth guard dangled off to the side of his helmet. He reached forward, to the gyroscopically mounted bottle holder, and took a short draw of beer. The bottle hadn't cracked but the beer was mostly foam. Otis's cheeks puffed out as he exhaled and got his bearings. He cautiously peered over the sides of the mower. If he hadn't seen evidence of sap and broken bark ahead of him, the skinned branch behind, and the fragrant smell of fresh-cut redwood, he'd have thought he was levitating. He wiggled his ass in the bucket seat. It seemed secure.

"You alright?" Marvin yelled. He wasn't quite sure what to do. Fifteen feet was considerably taller than any ladder he had.

"Could you chuck me up a Lucky?"

"Sure."

As Otis downed the extremely refreshing brew, his thoughts settled. His gaze fixed on the cooler, which housed more beers. He x-ray eyed them thirstily.

"You alright? Concussion? Anything?" Marvin queried.

Otis felt vivid. He knew it wasn't a dream as he slowly moved each set of bones deliberately to feel if anything had been broken. He hit the kill switch for the engine.

"I think I just got a couple bruises," Otis said.

* * *

Otis believed in dreams. Five years before, one had made him a moderately rich man with an enormous yellow truck with green hoses coiled on one side. Many human beings may be shaped by what they hate, but it was evident that Otis was shaped by what his wife hated: prairie dogs.

Well, that's a downright lie. She didn't mind the prairie dogs. She hated their holes in her lawn, but they were part and parcel.

The dream had come when Otis was in Marvin's garage. Their Team Turtlespeed lawnmower's engine was taken apart. Under the fluorescent lights, it sparkled like a Newtonian universe on the workbench; an ordered constellation of mechanics waiting to work right and follow exact rules. As Otis vacuumed up the metal shavings with the shop vac, he stopped, looked at the machine, lifted up his shirt, and stuck the nozzle to one of his man tits. After Otis let out a long yelp, jumped to turn the vacuum off, and suffered a three-inch diameter hickey centered over his nipple, the hose fell to the ground. He smiled as he looked up to see that Marvin had yanked the cord.

Marvin was used to Otis being a free spirit. Such behavior wasn't out of the ordinary. "What's got your brain crankin', chief?"

"Could we make a bigger shop vac?"

"How big?" Marvin asked.

Otis made some gestures with his hands, cupping and squeezing, but couldn't get the size right. Then he said, "Big enough to handle a prairie dog."

Marvin grinned and chuckled. "I'm sure it's possible."

Unfolding, as if in a dream, but very clean, linear, and real, everything fell quickly into place. The water district was selling a truck used to clean out sewer lines and manholes. It was reasonably priced and worked fine. The high school was selling their foam pole vault pits. The hoses were on sale at an industrial supply store, seemingly custom made for prairie dog suckage. Four inches wide. One weekend later, Marvin made the necessary modifications to the truck. It was much easier than making a land speed lawnmower, that was damn sure.

The rig worked like a charm. Both men knelt down in a testing field. Like doctors monitoring a stethoscope, they gently touched the hose which had been stuck down a prairie dog hole. Pebbles and small rocks rattled through. The hose shuddered, then got really still.

"I think we got one," Otis said. "It's fighting."

Marvin imagined the largest milkshake he'd ever drank, and stuck at the tip of the straw was a large piece of pineapple. The hose jolted wildly.

"Here it comes!" Otis screamed.

The prairie dog flumed through the hose and launched into the truck, where the other end of the hose was attached. The prairie dog bounced around on the inside of the truck, which had been softened by all the foam of the pole vault pits. They turned off the vacuum, opened the back door, and saw their captive a little dazed, but very much scampering around.

Success.

"He's a cute little guy," Otis said.

"He can be cute somewhere else," Marvin replied.

Later on that evening, under the cover of darkness and under the guise of scientific inquiry, Marvin fashioned a coupler that allowed the vacuum suction to be re-routed from the back of the truck while the other end was down a prairie dog hole.

Marvin radar gunned the prairie dog at three hundred miles per hour as it soared in an arc far over his head and plooped into a not-too-adjacent lake.

"I'm sure they can swim," Otis said, beaming.

"They sure as hell can fly pretty well," Marvin said as he saluted the too-far-to-be-seen prairie dog.

Otis's wife, whose only previous exposure to the men's new experiment was a massive hickey on her husband's boob, was rightfully skeptical when they unveiled the device to her. Five prairie dogs in twenty minutes, all alive, sucked from under the front yard and into the back of the truck, made her a believer. She smiled broadly, keeping her hands over the massive sound-blocking earmuffs on her head.

Otis had found a new, lucrative business. He landed full-time accounts with the local tribes, high school, and city works. Even do-gooder environmentalists begrudgingly liked what he did and admitted it was better than poisoning the rodents.

* * *

"Marvin, bring the truck around," Otis said. "The keys are in it."

Marvin snapped his fingers in a way that meant, "I should have thought of that earlier." He parked the truck about fifteen feet away from the trunk of the tree, opened up the back, pulled out the pole vault mat that was secured on the floor, then wiped off all the rocks and dirt. He looked up and placed it directly under Otis.

"That should do it. Don't stiffen up when you land, otherwise you'll bounce off."

Otis wanted to steel his nerve. "Chuck me another beer."

The flight path from Marvin's hand to Otis's couldn't have been more practiced between a pitcher and catcher. Otis caught the lobbed beer, drank it in three sucks, and hurtled the empty towards his recycle bin. It smashed against the side of his friend's house. Without further deliberation, he rolled out of the lawnmower to his left and fell like a bear hit by a tranquilizer dart onto the mat below. Upon contact, he belched and farted loudly, rolled off the mat, and got to his feet. The lawnmower listed severely to the right. Both men watched it hang there in fresh disbelief.

"You don't see a lawnmower in a tree every day," Otis said,

"especially that high."

At that, the mower fell in a slight twirl, landed upside down on the mat, bounced very high, and ended on the ground, wheels down, plaintively jiggling in its beefed-up suspension.

They stared at it incredulously.

"You okay?" Marvin asked.

Otis looked at his middle finger. "I think it's broke from the steering knob. Got it stuck in the middle of the wheel when it was turning. Think I got some bruises from the seatbelt, too. My shoulders hurt."

In measured paces, Marvin walked from the trunk of the tree over to the launch site. Calculations—numbers, symbols, weights, gravity, atmosphere—all cascaded in front of him. Physics.

"Fuck me," Marvin said.

Otis raised an eyebrow.

"Fuck me," Marvin said again. "I'll have to measure more accurately, but if my figures are correct, you were going a hundred miles an hour, give or take a couple." Marvin was rarely too far off. Calculators seemed to solely reaffirm his guesses.

Both men smiled, knowing they'd bested their best. They, unofficially, had the world's fastest lawnmower.

Marvin walked over to the lawnmower, reached down, and yanked its cord. It started right up. He flicked the throttle. It roared. He turned it off.

"Let's get that finger looked at," Marvin said. "We've got a full weekend coming up and I need you healthy. I'll start working on straightening up the chassis tomorrow."

"I'll get us some new tires," Otis replied, as he hopped in the passenger's seat.

"Glad you're okay," Marvin said. "You could have got real fucked up."

"Don't I know it."

"'I'm going to decimate you to the color of fuck'?" Marvin asked. "What was that about?"

"I was scared. I wanted to yell something. It sounded tough. What do you scream at a tree? I was caught off guard," Otis said. "All I'm hoping for tonight is a bubble bath and a blow job."

"That," Marvin smiled, "I can understand."

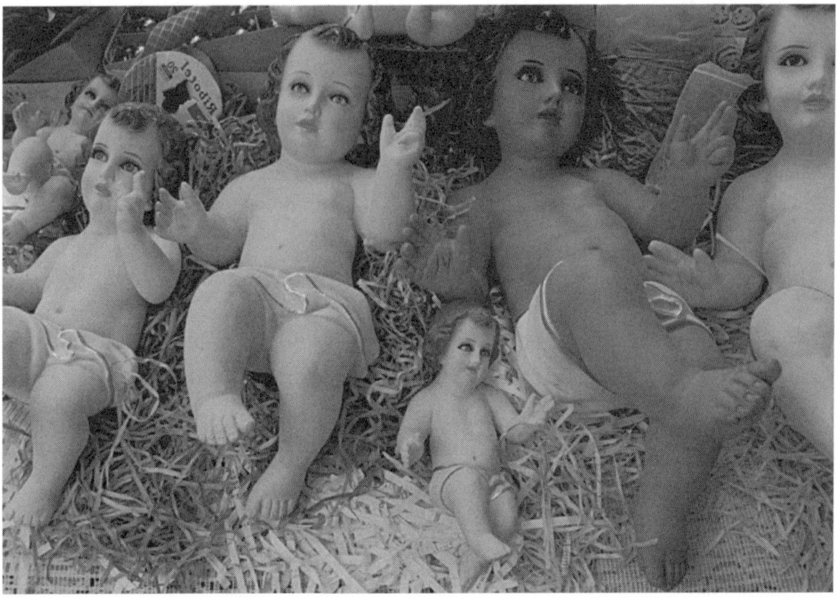

# The Undercards Trilogy

James Jay

*I. High Imperialism*

The forearm-long dolls being fobbed off as Kachinas wear RW on the heel of the right foot. RW, Roy Wertowski, junior high Social Studies teacher, retired, Bobcats football coach, retired, a big round man who tools with scraps of wood and canvas and sells the results in county fairs. But he's not in on this scam. Or is he? You tell me. Here's how it goes.

A small Navajo man, (who won't even whisper his own name anymore), his hands broken into hooks over the years, picks the dolls up at the fairs and sells them by his series of hand-painted highway signs that read "Don't Miss the Chief," then "Here's the Chief," then "Stop You've Missed Us," then "Friendly Indians Behind You. Turn Back." From the side of the road and surrounded by these signs, he takes in bills and coins and peels back the change one paper at a time, one coin at a time, saying nothing, and folks pull over to use his outhouse, stretch their legs, let their dogs run, or eye the tables of trinkets and rugs. Looking for sparks, colors, textures to imitate in his garage, Wertowski one day stops in and spots the RW dolls. He picks one up, rolls it over his big fingers and palm. He likes it. Something about the light out there, perhaps, the red dust over the plywood table, or the rez dogs and coyotes just over the brush eyeing the collared poodles, or maybe he just doesn't want any trouble, so he likes the dolls there, and at the next county fair he simply doubles his prices, they both nod on it, and the man with the hooked hands doubles his prices.

So is Roy Wertowski in on it? What about the man with the hooked hands? Well, I don't know. I can tell you this. I stopped by his place on the side of the road for a stretch, got out, walked, saw the shitting poodles, the folks in line for the outhouse, a handful of people combing the blankets and necklaces, saw the dolls, swore the last *official* sign I saw read "Navajo Nation," and I closed in on what looked like shards of a Barbie wardrobe over balsa, pine, and ironwood stuck together under a veil of tan, white, and black paints. Flipping the dolls, tugging the capes, lifting the cloth, I spotted my fingers being watched by the man while his hooks finished slowly making change for the customer in front of him. I extended the doll, began to speak, but on my arm he placed his hand, surprisingly gentle for such a mangled thing, and I could hear a laugh, maybe just a breath, barely audible in the dry air, and he gave me the doll for nothing. Now, I don't know if I'm in on it, but at home I keep the doll on a prominent shelf and from such a height hear stories.

### *II. Miles of Dirt to Cover*

*for Ron French*

He tailed us for hours through the summer heat of long, straight Texas roads. And you, who I'd known only a year, drove while my mother sat quiet in the front seat and my brother and I made small shifts to look behind. You sped up our car, slowed us down, pulled over once, but the man pulled off behind us and waited. You pulled back on the road. Sped up. What else was there to do? The man swerved out after us and followed so close that from our back seat I could sneak glances of his face drenched in sweat, the straight edges of his cheeks, the dirty brown layers of coat, on flannel, on T-shirt, his large hands gripping the wheel.

You whipped us over again, quicker. The man, forced to pull over in front, waited about forty yards ahead. I don't remember seeing how you got there, but you were half way to his car and walked in long strides with your .357 held straight down on your right side. You closed. I propped my head over the front seat and squinted. The man sat still. You stopped just behind his door. I could not hear what was said, but it was just a few seconds, then you let him go.

A few hours down the road we stopped at a two story motel, and I laid awake in bed beside my brother; our bodies still small enough to fit in a single. Under thin sheets I wished you had shot the man. I imagined the car headlights peering through the dark, you tracking him all night, catching up to him at daybreak in a truck stop diner. I could see your arm raised and your revolver pointing as straight as the horizon shining into his numb face. I wanted to know that man's head had been leveled, clean from his shoulders, blown apart and the pieces a mess of nothing. I didn't want it to be like a movie where the good guy lets the bad guy go with a warning, until the bad guy blows it again, and the white hat has to be put back on and miles of dirt covered before the last showdown. I wanted to fast forward to the scene where the boy, who fetches water and ropes and other small but useful things, thanks the hero, comes up with the right line or two to say, the well-timed tear, the sun light pin-pointing the grass, the magic that glues it all together, but this was no film where we stew and spin above miranda days. I had no words, right ones or wrong, but you stayed anyway and knew what to level and what not to level and I say thank you, late.

## *III. Captain Rowe*

Captain Rowe was like a fist. His bald head wide and continually stern, his neck and shoulders slabs of meat, barrel chested, a shade under six feet tall, he made his way through the world with heavy heel toe steps.

Currently, the United States Army assigned Captain Rowe to Kentucky to work on computers, his thick fingers writing program one day after the next. He'd been in fourteen years and was looking for one of the early retirement routes, just needed to work the numbers out. He'd been promised early retirement for years, then they ran out of those slots, then he could have a prorated deal, then… and then they went on and on. Whatever drew Captain Rowe to the Army had long since died. It got him through school, got him out of the country for a while, moved him around enough so that great, lonely air in the middle of even the tightest fist never had time to think about what it didn't get to touch.

He used theater to map where he'd been in his Army career. Shakespeare was his primary marker, although he'd see the occasional Marlowe play and had caught a Ben Johnson Festival in Eugene, Oregon. His years in Flagstaff, Arizona were highlighted by the University's three plays per year. Always the staple of *Romeo and Juliet* and *A Midsummer Night's Dream*, but the repetition never bothered him. The students were sincere, hardworking, if not convincing. Flagstaff also had a small independent theater, Theatrikos, which was irregular but surprising with its performances. In diners alone, he recalled the excellent acoustics of its 100 chair auditorium. Butte, Montana helped him with its Irish Everlast Theater Company switching from the staple of plays by Yeats, Wilde, Beckett, and doing *King Lear* for two weeks in February when the temperature never rose above zero. Spokane, Washington was the worst; Postmodern confusion was the only thing stirring in the University and no local action. The low budget, in the park, single scene efforts of Smith, South Dakota charmed him. Thin-voiced men shouting soliloquies to the trees, water paint backdrops falling on top of unfazed actors, the cardboard sword bending at all the wrong times. In Kentucky, Captain Rowe fed himself on a staple of BBC videos from the library and hoped for the best. He knew it wouldn't be enough.

Flagstaff, Arizona and the calling of what might be showing may have drove him AWOL as much as anything else, that drama down the road, hard to say about these things. What breaks a man? Can a man only be broken when he wants to be? Captain Rowe packed his GMC with ten evenly sized boxes: eight of which contained his video collection, one more for CDs and cassettes, one for books. With him in the cab, he kept his laptop, boom box, television, VCR player (he never bothered investing in DVD—he knew the trend wouldn't last as long as 8 track). The truck packed, he finished the last two beers in the refrigerator, then spread a gallon of gasoline throughout his one bedroom apartment located in the packed dirt lot behind the Catholic church. The smell of fumes followed him out the doorway. A pitch of a match and up it went, and out of Kentucky the Captain drove, heading to your town.

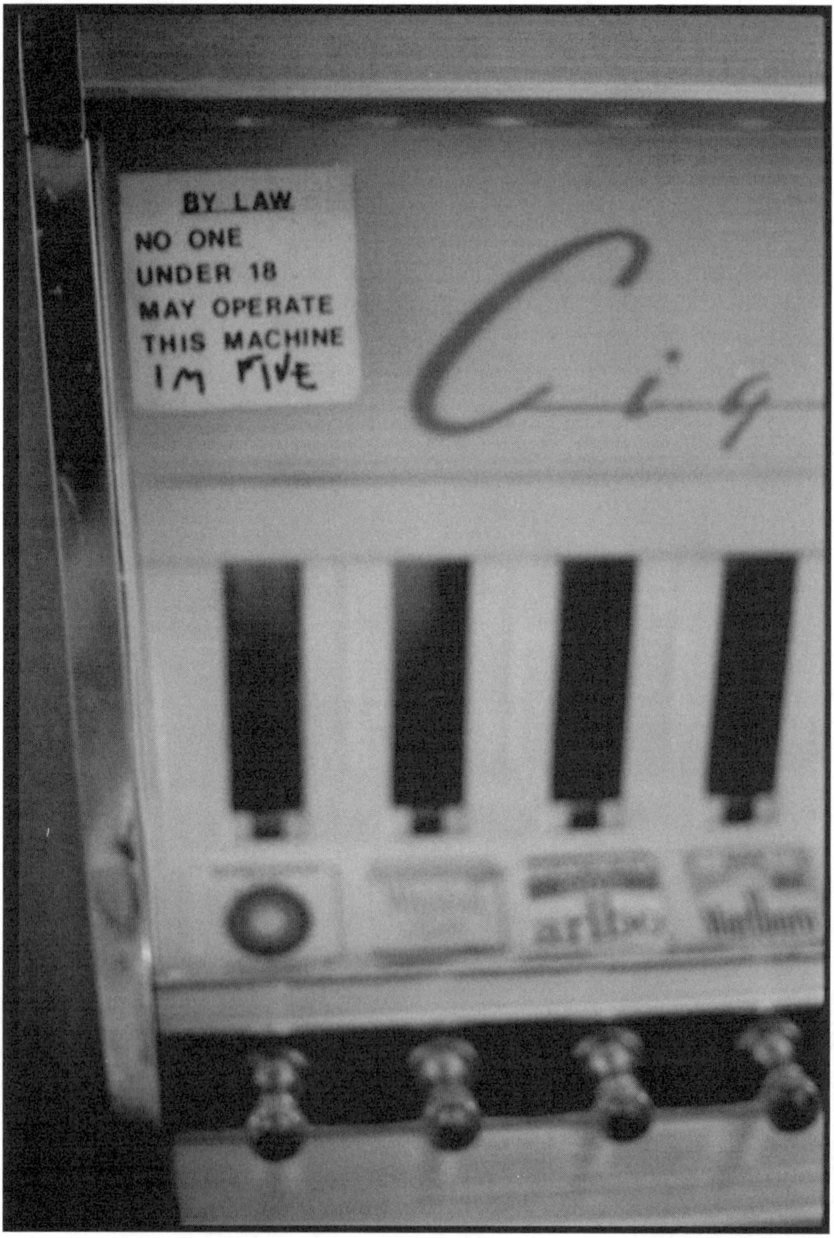
BY LAW
NO ONE
UNDER 18
MAY OPERATE
THIS MACHINE
IM FIVE

# Smashing

Felizon Vidad

"Tell me why I should go tonight," Lenore said to Jinx. She started the car, a sagging old Cutlass that Jinx liked to call Futless. Futless was thirteen years old, poor thing. Futless was also paid for in full, so Lenore wasn't complaining.

"Do I need to give you a reason?" Jinx buckled her seat belt and grinned at the styrofoam takeout box that she held in her lap. "Check it out. Two dozen hot wings for ten cents a wing. We got dinner here for under three bucks."

Last week, one of the other dental hygienists had told Jinx about happy hour at D'Albora's off Indian River Road. Four-dollar pitchers of Bud and ten-cent wings from five to seven, Thursday and Friday nights. Jinx didn't care about the beer as much as she cared about the wings. She figured she could order a couple dozen, nibble on one or two wings, then tell the bartender that she was full and could she have the rest wrapped up to go?

That was the plan, and Lenore had grudgingly gone along with it this Friday afternoon. It wasn't a bad plan, really, because she and Jinx were going to take the leftover wings home and eat them up for dinner with a pot of steamed white rice. It was a joke among their friends that Filipinos ate everything with rice. Lenore and Jinx just didn't let on how much of it was actually true.

"Don't change the subject," Lenore said. She pulled out of the dirt parking lot and slowly maneuvered the car towards 520 East, headed for Cocoa Beach. Even though it was nearly seven and the sun was an hour away from setting, the air remained thick and humid. It pressed against their faces, heavy around their shoulders like a dampened hot towel. It would be cooler once they got closer to the ocean.

"Give me one good reason, Jinx. Tell me why I should go."

"I'm not changing the subject," Jinx said petulantly. "I just think it would be nice if you went with me to Camilla Christopher's bachelorette party. Why?" She began to tick off the reasons. "Because you're my roommate… Because you're a blood relative… Because you love me… And because there'll be a lot of free food… A lot of free drinks… And you won't have to fork over a single dime."

Jinx knew exactly where to get her. Lenore was constantly broke, trying to pay back her student loans and the credit card bills that she'd racked up in college. She barely made enough money as a substitute teacher now, and her cousin knew it.

"Okay. But then there's the bridal shower, and I always have to buy a bridal shower gift," Lenore countered. They neared the major intersection in front of the Merritt Square Mall. On this early Friday evening, traffic was not as congested as it would have been a few months ago, during the snowbird season. Lenore slowed to a stop as the light turned yellow. Poor Futless could not be counted on to run a yellow light. The car shook noticeably as it idled.

"Forget about the bridal shower!" Jinx said. "I'll get a gift. You can put your name on my card. I'm telling you, you won't have to pay a dime if you come out tonight. Will you just go to this damn bachelorette party with me? Please."

Lenore didn't believe her for one second about not having to pay a dime. Especially if the bachelorette party ended in any one of the downtown Cocoa Beach bars. She couldn't understand why this was so important to Jinx, anyway. Camilla Christopher had been Jinx's childhood friend and next-door neighbor, not hers.

"What's the gift?" she demanded.

Jinx looked baffled. "What gift?"

"The bridal shower gift."

"What does it matter? You're not paying for it."

"Yes, but it'll matter if I put my name on it."

"Aha! So you're saying you'll come to the bachelorette party?"

The light changed to green. Lenore got the car rolling again and glanced at her cousin. Jinx had opened the takeout box and was now deeply inhaling the wet, spicy smell of hot chicken wings.

"Hey! Cut that out. Don't breathe your germs all over it."

"I can't help it," Jinx said and sighed heavily, right into the open box of hot wings. "Ahhhh... It smells so good."

"Too bad. Can't you wait? We'll be home in a few minutes."

Jinx sighed again and made a lot of noise trying to tuck the styrofoam lid shut. "Will you please just go with me tonight to Camilla's bachelorette party? She's expecting one, she's even named it, and she'll be pissed if no one shows up."

"That's why you want me to go, isn't it?"

"What?"

"You want me to go so there'll be one more body there. So it won't be so empty. Right? You just need me to fill in the space."

They were making the gradual ascent over the 520 bridge into Cocoa Beach. The flat glass of the Banana River stretched out on either side of them. Jinx turned her head and studied the row of homes and condos that receded south along the mirrored line of the river.

"I'm just a *body* to fill in the space," Lenore said bitterly.

Jinx didn't say anything.

"It doesn't matter what I *think* or what I *feel*. You just want me there to stand around like a dummy, so Camilla Christopher will feel like she has a whole lot of friends. I'd rather stay home."

Jinx was done being patient. This was nearly a record for her. Two minutes.

"For chrissake, Lenore!" she snapped. The box of hot wings nearly slipped off her lap. "Truth is, I wanted you to come out tonight because all you ever do lately is sit around and watch TV. You never want to leave the house or do anything anymore. It's been three weeks. You're letting yourself get too depressed for your own damn good."

Jinx glared out the window. Lenore pressed her lips tightly together and kept driving, making herself concentrate on keeping the car centered exactly on her side of the road. Even though Jinx hadn't said it, they both knew what she meant. When a guy doesn't call you for over three weeks, you've got to know that it's over. Lenore just hadn't gotten around to saying it out loud yet.

Neither one of them spoke. They drove past more condos and turned left onto A1A. The stretch over the Banana River had been a brief reprieve. Here was a fresh assault of various shades of lurid pink buildings, squashed up one next to the other like oversized sand castles. Chain restaurants, motels and hotels, intermittently punctuated by tourist trap surf stores that sold the predictable seashells and sharks' teeth. It was officially Cocoa Beach. Lenore stuck her arm out the window and wiggled her fingers in the breeze.

Jinx broke the silence first. "So maybe that was a little harsh. I'm sorry."

"It's okay." Lenore had already decided it would be stupid to get upset with Jinx.

"I guess you don't want to talk about it?"

"No. I don't."

"Okay." Jinx glanced out the window and remembered what had started all this. "I told you Camilla came up with a name for her stupid bachelorette party, didn't I? She's calling it the *Countdown to My Wedding BP*."

"Huh." Lenore forced a laugh. "*Countdown to My Wedding*. That's a lame ass name. And we can only assume that 'BP' stands for 'bachelorette party', right?"

"What can I tell you? Camilla is a lame ass."

"Who *names* their bachelorette party? Jeez, what a geek."

"I know," Jinx said. "It's typical Camilla."

"Typical Camilla," Lenore repeated.

Futless chugged on. They were only a few blocks away from home now, and Lenore would have liked to sail through all green lights from that point on. She was afraid that one of these days, she would be sitting at a stop light, and poor Futless would just refuse to go on. She hoped it wouldn't be at this particular intersection they were approaching, in front of Shoreline Plaza, the recently built shopping center that took up probably the last bit of undeveloped land left on Cocoa Beach. Shoreline was just another excuse for more shops that rented out kayaks and surfboards, more boutiques that sold expensive sunblock and cheap Hawaiian print beachwear. As if there weren't enough tourist traps within a half-mile radius. At least there was that one good thing about the hot weather and summer months: fewer snowbirds, less traffic.

Waiting for the light to change, Lenore thought about Camilla Christopher, who was twenty-two and always wore chiffon scarves that matched the color of her pantsuits and strappy high heeled sandals. Camilla worked as a receptionist in Cape Canaveral, mostly answering phones for a real estate office, but she dressed like a power career woman in expensive clothes that she charged on her father's credit card. No one knew exactly what career Camilla hoped to pursue, because she had stopped going to college after her second year in Gainesville and she never officially declared a major. What everyone *did* know was that Camilla was on her way to getting married and becoming a stay-at-home You-Would-Thinker. It was already well established in Merritt Island that Camilla's mother was one of those.

In high school, Lenore and Jinx had attended Camilla's sixteenth birthday party at the Cocoa Beach Country Club. The place swarmed with money and the snotty attitude that comes with it. Lenore had retreated to a corner where she could watch everyone else and still be near the hors d'oeuvres. Jinx stood next to her and ate a handful of honey roasted peanuts, one piece at a time. Camilla's mother, who was circulating the room and making small talk, wandered over to the buffet table, picked up a small plate, and assessed the spread critically.

Her hair was freshly permed and frosted, and she wore a bright yellow suit with huge matching earrings and pendant.

"Nice citrines," Jinx commented.

"Yellow diamonds," Mrs. Christopher corrected her. "Hello, darlings. How *are* you?"

"Fine," Lenore said.

"Never been better," Jinx said.

"Smashing," Mrs. Christopher said and smiled a phony smile that showed laser-bleached white teeth. "How are your parents, Lenore?"

"They're fine," Lenore answered, but Camilla's mother was nodding in a way that showed she wasn't listening at all. "They'll keep running the restaurant until the day they die, but other than that, they're fine."

"That's nice," Mrs. Christopher said, surveying the room and frowning. "Tell them hello for me. I love your mother's *pancit* dish. Oh, for crying out loud. Are we out of the shrimp rolls? Where is my party planner? Why is she not taking care of this? For all that money we're paying her, you would think she'd at least refill the pretzel bowls."

"Yeah," Jinx said, lifting a hand to pop the last peanut in her mouth. She squinted at Mrs. Christopher's yellow diamonds and stared at the one that sat like a golden egg fastened to her skinny neck. "Yeah, you *would* think."

Camilla Christopher, Lenore decided, already looked like her mother.

Of course, she couldn't confirm this for sure until Camilla showed up for the bachelorette party.

It was nearly eleven o'clock. Not even an hour had passed since Lenore and Jinx had arrived at Melissa Goldman's house. Melissa Goldman was hosting the *Countdown to My Wedding BP*. The party was to begin at Melissa's place, Jinx had explained, and then everyone would walk over to the bars a couple of blocks away in downtown Cocoa Beach.

Lenore knew she was trapped for the evening. Like it or not, she would be a participating member of the *Countdown to My Wedding BP*. To stay at home again tonight would only confirm what Jinx already thought: that she was letting some guy control the way she lived her life. Duane hadn't called in three weeks, four days. She didn't know anymore if she cared. Only a couple of hours ago, she'd been home, ensconced in the comfort of the old brown corduroy recliner, enjoying hot wings with a bowl of steamed white rice, dripping the spicy sauce everywhere and happily watching yet another cooking show on Food Network. Now she sat on a bar stool pulled up to someone else's kitchen counter, staring at an unappetizing assortment of store-bought chips and homogenized dips in bland, white containers. She could barely conceal her boredom.

Someone tuned the crackling stereo to the seventies disco station, and someone else started to dance like she was on *Saturday Night Fever*. Lenore recognized the song about ringing my bell. One girl, Tammy, was especially enthusiastic. She wore a leopard-print tube dress that fit her like a body stocking, and she didn't dance so much as ooze sexuality. She shimmied her lower body, thrust her breasts forward, squatted and gyrated. A lap dance for an invisible seated man.

*The night is young and full of possibilities, well come on and let yourself be free…*

Tammy pretended to hold a bell aloft in her right hand and shook her body along.

"You can ring my behh-ehh-ell, ring my bell… my bell, ring-a-ling-a-ling…"

Tammy spun in a little circle, oblivious, or uncaring, or simply drunk. She whirled helicopter-style with arms outstretched, fingers spread wide, and Lenore noticed the thin pale line of a missing wedding band, a contrast against the girl's dark tan.

A few feet away, their backs turned to the impromptu dance floor, Jinx, Melissa Goldman, and a tall, dark-haired girl named Jackie made small talk as they waited for the rest of the guests to show up. Lenore shifted her bar stool a little closer to Jinx, to make it appear as if she were part of the conversation. She needed to stop staring at Tammy.

"If you think so, go ahead," Jackie was saying.

Jinx pretended to lean over for a handful of tortilla chips. "If you're wondering about Tammy," she whispered, "homegirl's got an eleven-month-old baby and a rich hubby in South Merritt Island."

"Oh, I don't mind," Jackie said. "You can check them if you want."

Melissa removed Jackie's glasses from her face. She held the frames up to the light and inspected the lens. "I don't know, these look kind of funny to me. This one side is not the same as the other."

Jinx took a sip of her Mountain Dew and raised an eyebrow at Lenore.

"They seem all right to me." Jackie shrugged. "They're

supposed to be the same on both sides."

"If you think her glasses are funny," Lenore offered, an attempt to join the conversation, "you should try on my glasses. I have one nearsighted and one farsighted prescription. If you put them on, they'd seem all funky."

Melissa Goldman blinked and looked at Lenore as if she had suddenly materialized on that bar stool like uninvited rabbit turd. "Oh, you don't know who you're talking to. I'm an optician."

Jinx, who had just taken another sip, coughed on her drink. Lenore felt her cheeks grow hot. She wasn't an ignorant foreigner, but Melissa certainly acted as if she'd just arrived fresh off the boat. For all the pompousness in her voice, Melissa might as well have said, "Do you know how to speak English?"

Instantly, Lenore disliked Melissa, hated her limp dirty-blonde hair and the ferrety face that was all sharpness and angles.

Jinx opened her mouth to say something, but at that moment, there came the sound of scuffling outside Melissa's front door. In another minute, Camilla Christopher and two other girls burst in, giggling and breathless. They seemed a tangle of big hair and short skirts, helium mylar balloons and curly ribbons, all wrapped up in the stems of long yellow roses and white carnations.

"Hello, dolls!" Camilla cried to nobody in particular. Apparently, she'd already consumed several pre-party drinks. Her normally sharp, fashion plate clothes, hair, and makeup seemed smudged. The vision of perfection, smeared like a bleary windshield. Someone smirked. Melissa set Jackie's eyeglasses on the counter and rushed forward to help unwind ribbons and disentangle the flowers.

"What was *that* all about?" Jinx hissed at Lenore's elbow. She imitated Melissa's haughty expression. "'Oh, you don't know who you're talking to!'"

"I'm not sure," Lenore murmured back, "but don't let me get drunk, or I may kill that girl."

"Okay, everybody!" Melissa called out. She clapped her hands for attention. "The bride-to-be is here! It's scavenger hunt time!"

Camilla stood in the center of the room, a goofy smile on her face and a handful of carnations and curly ribbons in her fist. Someone turned down the volume on the stereo. Tammy stopped dancing and pouted, shifting her weight from one leopard-print platform sandal to the other. The room grew quiet. Apparently, this was the extent of the number of guests. Lenore counted eleven people, including herself, and wondered if anyone here was really a friend of Camilla Christopher's. Or Melissa Goldman's.

"The girls and I put together a scavenger hunt for you," Melissa said grandly, in the manner of a philanthropist bestowing a million-dollar bridal gift. Lenore tried to determine who "the girls" were. Certainly, neither she nor Jinx had anything to do with this scavenger hunt. From the bewildered looks on the faces of the other "girls," it appeared that no one had known about it, either. Melissa had to be talking about herself and her multiple personalities.

"Oh, goody!" Camilla exclaimed and let go of the curly ribbons. Carnations dropped to the floor, and the helium mylar balloons to which the ribbons were attached floated gently to the ceiling. "Where's the list?"

With an ostentatious flourish, Melissa produced a folded piece of paper from her back hip pocket. Jinx nudged Lenore and rolled her eyes.

Camilla unfolded the list and tapped a French-manicured nail tip against her even, white teeth. Up until then, Lenore had never seen anyone read out loud and smile wide at the same time. Camilla was better than a ventriloquist.

"*Collect or accomplish the following things in any number and combination of bars in the local area.*" Even under the influence of alcohol, Camilla could do a dramatic read-aloud and best any middle school reading teacher in the county.

"The choice is yours," Melissa explained. "If you choose not to do what it says on the list, then you have to do a shot."

She turned to the rest of the women in the room and said, "If it were me, I think I'd just take the shots."

Yeah, Lenore thought, but it ain't you.

"Oh, I'm game," Camilla said. She returned to her list. "*One, get a Blow Job shot and drink it between a guy's legs.* I can do that. *Two, kiss a bald man on his head.*"

"Which head?" Tammy hollered, and everyone in the room cracked up. Camilla didn't even blush or wait for the laughter to stop.

"*Three, ask a married man for advice.* What would I ask? *Four, get a condom from a man.* Does it matter what kind? *Five, obtain a man's boxers or underwear. Last, get on top of a bar and dance.*" Camilla looked up and clutched the list to her chest. "I love it! This is great! I want to do the Blow Job first!"

"We should get going, then," Jinx said.

Lenore hopped off the bar stool and reached for her brown crocheted purse. The bars closed at two, but the sooner they got started, maybe the sooner she'd get home.

Outside, the night air was cool, wide and open. Pinpricks of starlight dotted the inky wash of sky. On a beautiful summer night like this, the ocean so close and the sky curving broadly overhead like a giant's deep, upside-down bowl, you could lose yourself. Lenore felt like she could be Tammy for a moment, whirling in a circle, arms extended to embrace the world. Inhibitions gone, the physical body forgotten.

*The night is young and full of possibilities, well come on and let yourself be free...*

"Let me see your scarf, honey," Melissa said. "That's beautiful."

Lenore had been lagging behind everybody, catching bits of other people's conversations. Jinx was ahead, talking to Jackie and another woman named Ellabeth. Closest to Lenore were Camilla and Melissa, walking slowly because of their ridiculously high heels.

The scarf, a design of opaque white flowers on sheer white chiffon, fluttered like a ghostly streamer as Camilla handed it over. Melissa wound the shimmery fabric around her own neck, carelessly tossing the end over a shoulder. She stopped walking, put both hands on her waist and jutted out her left hip, posing like a fashion model.

Coming up from behind, Lenore imagined herself catching just a corner of the chiffon and yanking as hard as she could. She pictured Melissa's knees buckling under, her ankles twisting on those ridiculously expensive and impractical high heels, arms groping for balance, eyes wide open in surprise. Popping in the strain of suffocation.

"Are you thinking about Duane?"

Jinx's face appeared a few inches away, looming just above Lenore's right shoulder. Lenore shook the drowsy haze that had settled over her like fine mosquito netting. She'd been drifting off, sitting in this noisy, crammed bar that Camilla had chosen. They'd all been sitting at that sticky round table for what seemed like hours, but it had probably been only twenty minutes. There were no clocks in the place. The décor was a clash of sports bar and seafood restaurant: assorted pro football posters and Florida State Seminoles paraphernalia amid stuffed mounted marlins and old-fashioned rope fishing nets spread out and tacked up against the walls. Each wooden table was topped by a slab of clear resin that had been poured over carefully arranged designs of seashells on sand. It was just another Cocoa Beach raw bar, full of college boys and working class men, yuppie You-Would-Thinkers, and aging beach bunnies who still insisted on wearing acid wash miniskirts, bleaching their already straw-like hair, and tanning to the texture of an old leather handbag. It was the kind of place where the servers were stick-limbed girls with big boobs, all tanned skin and tight little shorts, tight little tops, and they expected you to kiss their feet for being so beautiful—even the homely ones (which happened to be most of them). If you didn't, or if you were a boisterous group of women with one very drunk bride-to-be, your chances of getting refills were considerably cut.

Lenore sipped her nearly warm beer and became keenly aware of the bad rock music from the jukebox; from behind the bar, the smash of glass bottles pitched against more glass; and movement, the hubbub of a packed bar on a summer night in Cocoa Beach. The feeling that life was swirling in eddies around her, and she stood still, invisible, in the middle of it all.

"No," she said, "I'm not thinking about Duane."

"You look like you're off in another world," Jinx told her.

"I'm okay," Lenore said.

Camilla's Blow Job arrived in a tall, narrow shot glass, frothy on top with whipped cream. The other women in the group hooted and howled. Their server, a petite blonde girl with long, straight hair, placed the shot glass carefully in front of Camilla and backed off as if she expected it to explode. Camilla lowered her head and darted the tip of her tongue into the whipped cream. Tammy pounded her hand on the table and screamed with laughter. Lenore saw nothing funny about it, wished it could all be over and she was back at home.

"You've got to down it between some guy's legs!" Melissa called out across the table.

Camilla extended her thumb and forefinger like a crab's claw and, daintily, she lifted the shot glass with pinky finger extended. "Who should I do?"

"That one over there is pretty hot," Tammy suggested, pointing at the end of the bar towards a tall guy with short, curly brown hair. He was deeply engaged in conversation with a very skinny girl wearing a baseball cap.

"He's with a girl!" Camilla exclaimed.

"Oh, don't let it stop you!" Tammy said. "He's mighty fine. Want me to go ask him?"

Camilla giggled. "Why don't you come with me to go ask him?"

The two of them got up and bumped into an older man in a cowboy hat. He wasn't very tall; the heels on his cowboy boots didn't make much of a difference. Camilla and Tammy looked down at his boots and let their eyes travel up the rest of his cowboy outfit, then looked at each other and burst into laughter. The Blow Job shot in Camilla's hand sloshed dangerously close to Jinx's head, but most of the drink stayed in the glass. Jinx didn't notice.

Apparently, the man in the cowboy hat thought Camilla and Tammy were just a couple of giggly girls. He smiled and nodded in a friendly manner, lurched a bit, tipped his hat, and let them pass. Lenore watched all this as one might gaze at the muted television in a doctor's office, not really giving it much thought, but the man didn't continue on his way. Instead, he stopped dead in front of the cousins and looked down at both of them.

"Hey, I know you!" the man in the cowboy hat exclaimed. He pointed a finger straight at Lenore and shook it. "Vietnam, 1963!"

It seemed all eyes had turned to look at her, and the jukebox had suddenly hushed. Lenore was horrified. Vietnam? What was this crazy fool talking about?

"Vietnam, 1963!"

"What the fuck are you talking about?" That was Jinx.

Jinx had always prided herself on their heritage, saying that Filipinos were part Asian and part Spanish, part of a rich culture and history. Apparently, the Asian part didn't include Vietnam.

The old man in the cowboy hat kept grinning, unsteady on his feet. His lips stretched out to reveal straight yellow teeth that were probably dentures. He continued to point at Lenore and shake his finger. Then he spotted Jinx and whirled to aim his finger at her, like a gunslinger who'd just whipped out on the draw. "Vietnam, 1963!" he crowed.

"He's drunk," Jackie whispered.

Across the table, Melissa called out, "What is he saying?"

Lenore wished she could disappear.

"Is this fucker telling us we look *Vietnamese*?" Jinx was furious.

"Pops!" Through the packed crowd, a young guy in a blue short-sleeved mechanic's work shirt was making his way over to their table. "Pops! Come on, time to go home."

The old man lifted an arm like a traffic signal, hand splayed to indicate *stop*, and with the other hand fumbled around in his pocket as if digging for change. He muttered to himself. Lenore stared helplessly, benumbed.

"Come on, Pops." The guy had the old man by the arm. "Time to go."

The old man found what he was looking for. The yellow teeth formed a crescent slice like cheese. He dropped a piece of paper into Lenore's lap, winked at her, and let his son tow him through the crowd and out the bar.

"What in hell was that all about?" Jinx demanded.

Camilla and Tammy had returned to the table, having successfully snagged the tall guy with the curly brown hair. He appeared through the maze of clustered standing bodies, minus his earlier baseball-capped female companion. Attention shifted from *Vietnam, 1963!* to the bride-to-be, her Blow Job shot, and the newest addition to their party. Lenore was more than happy to be forgotten.

In her lap was a worn and folded, yet most definitely genuine, hundred-dollar bill.

She realized that her mouth had been slightly agape this whole time. She shut it.

"Ladies, this is Willie," Camilla said. "Willie has very kindly agreed to help me achieve the first goal on my list."

Willie shook hands with everybody, even Tammy who had been standing right there when Camilla originally asked him for assistance. Tammy held Willie's hand several seconds longer than she needed to.

"Thanks for agreeing to do this, Willie," Tammy said warmly, as if this were her own bachelorette party being celebrated. "You're a sweetheart."

"My pleasure," Willie returned. "You're not so bad yourself."

Tammy couldn't have looked more thrilled. "Oh, you hardly *know* me."

"You certainly don't," Camilla put in. "She's a slut. Come on, Willie. Have a seat and let's get at it."

Tammy pouted, but it seemed no one but Lenore noticed. The rest were all too interested in Willie.

Willie straddled Camilla's vacated chair, and she positioned herself in front of him. All of the *BP* leaned forward to watch. Several others nearby looked on with curiosity.

Camilla took the shot glass with the Blow Job and fit it between Willie's thighs. Then she lowered herself to the dirty bar floor and kneeled at Willie's feet. Leaning forward with her hands behind her back, she approached the shot glass with what Lenore noted was an experienced air. Camilla knew exactly what to do and how to do it, as if she'd done this a million times.

Lenore tried to shake the disturbing thought of the You-Would-Think princess actually giving a blow job. But it was all so easy to picture, especially when Camilla bent over, her face in Willie's lap, and slowly fit her mouth around the rim of the narrow glass. Then, straightening, hands still clasped behind her, she tipped her head back and downed the Blow Job in one long, continuous swallow.

"Beautiful!" Willie applauded, and the rest of the onlookers joined in, hooting and cheering. Camilla pulled the shot glass out of her mouth with a loud *pop*, grinned widely, and made a sweeping bow.

"Might as well kill two birds with one stone," she said to Jackie, who was the closest. To Willie, she said, "Hey, one more thing. I need to get my hands on a guy's underwear."

Willie stood up. "I'd love to, honey, but I'm freeballing it tonight."

"Too bad," Camilla said, not bothering to feign disappointment. "Thanks anyway."

"My pleasure." Willie gave them all a little wave and took off.

Camilla sank into the empty chair. She suddenly looked very drunk and tired.

"You can't be done yet," Jackie told her. "You still have five more things on your list."

Melissa came around the table and hauled Camilla back to her feet. "Come on, chick. Let's go look for a married bald man so you can ask him for some condoms and advice."

"Mmm, mmm, that Willie," Tammy said when they were gone. "Hot stuff." She helped herself to the nearly empty pitcher of beer, pouring the rest of it into her glass.

"How's your husband doing?" Jinx asked.

"I wouldn't know," Tammy replied. "He isn't here." She laughed like she had told the funniest joke and then guzzled her beer.

Lenore looked at Tammy. Tammy's dark, shoulder-length bob, which had been moussed and blow-dried and sprayed artfully at the beginning of the evening, was now deflated and resembled frayed yarn. Gobby mascara caked in the corners of her eyes; the black eyeliner that traced both her upper and lower lids only created a raccoon effect.

Tammy drained the rest of her beer and slammed the glass down. Her face was starting to get that drunk, puffy look. When she turned to Lenore, her eyes squinched up as if she were staring at the sun. Lenore smiled at her pleasantly.

Suddenly, Tammy was transformed: she drew her lips back and raised her fingers like stiff claws. It was her simulation of an angry feline. "RrrrrrRRRRR! I'm a caged tiger on the loose, hear me roar!"

Jinx and Lenore looked at each other. Lenore suppressed the urge to laugh. Tammy rose from her chair, her hands still bent at the wrists in imitation of tiger claws, and pawed at the air like a crazed animal.

Jackie leaned over and remarked, as if to explain it all, "This is the first night in a long time that she's been out. Her mother-in-law is watching the baby."

"Where's her husband?" That was the only thing Lenore cared to know.

"Oh, most likely at home." Jackie checked to see if Tammy was paying attention and then said, "He's really a nice guy. Despite what others might say."

For a married woman who had an eleven-month-old child being babysat at home by her mother-in-law, Tammy looked and acted exactly that: a married woman with an eleven-month-old kid at home, being let out for one night of freedom with the single girls.

Lenore almost felt sorry for her.

It was hard to say at what point the bar had become extremely crowded, but it seemed that suddenly there were just too many people in the room. The music, the talking, the laughter—all of it was just a pounding, throbbing noise in her head.

She wondered vaguely if maybe, at home, the phone was ringing for her.

People were standing around where they could find room. Tammy, who had remained still in a sort of catlike trance, abruptly pushed her chair back, knocking it into two men who were holding a conversation behind her. Maybe it was an accident, but she'd succeeded in getting their attention.

"Hey, take it easy," the taller one said. He held his bottle of beer away, as if he expected her to strike again.

Tammy tilted her head and smiled flirtatiously. "I'm sorry, what's your name?"

The man looked startled, and Lenore could see why. Tammy was acting as if he had been coming on to her.

But the man recovered fast. He held out his hand to shake and said, "I'm Sal." He ticked his head sideways to motion at his friend. "This is Pete."

"A group of us are celebrating my friend's bachelorette party," Tammy informed them. She shook hands but didn't bother to introduce Jinx or Lenore, both sitting within earshot and obviously a part of her group. "What about you guys? Boys' night out?"

"Sure enough," said Pete. He wore a long-sleeved plaid flannel shirt, even though the number of bodies pressing around them had probably elevated the room temperature ten more degrees. "The ladyfolk are at home. How about you? Your bachelorette party coming up, too?"

Tammy swatted Pete playfully on the shoulder and laughed, making sure to throw her head back and draw attention to her breasts strapped tightly in their leopard-print sheath. "Oh, you! Please! I'm already married!" She laughed again.

If she pushed her chest any more forward, Lenore mused, she'd probably throw her back out.

"Tell me something," Tammy said, changing tack and dropping her voice to a conspiratorial tone. "Don't you guys ever feel trapped at home, being married and all? I mean, don't you ever just want to go out for one night and just say, screw it? Like just go, *Fuck it all!*"

"We *are* out," Sal said. "I don't know what you're getting at."

"Oh, come off it!" Tammy said. Her rimmed-black eyes squinched even smaller, and she swiftly got a mean look on her face. "You know what I'm talking about! You guys sit at home every night with your wives and kids until pretty soon, you're just wanting to get out! Like a caged tiger… waiting to jump out when you see the chance to escape. Looking to go on the prowl!"

Her hands were up again, fingers forming claws.

"Do you go out at night?" Pete demanded.

"No," Tammy said. Poised like that, she looked foolish, like a grown woman caught in a game of pretend.

"Do you make it a point to go out at least once a week with your friends?" Pete stepped closer to her. Lenore, sitting inches from his hip, could smell sweat, like a musty odor of cumin and chili powder, emanating from the plaid flannel.

"Do you?" the man repeated.

Tammy's arms dropped to her sides. She could only look at him, confused.

"No? Ever just have a beer? Kick back and talk about other things? You ever go out at all and just try to have a good time without your husband or your kid? Huh?"

Tammy took a step back. She whispered, barely audible, "No."

Pete swigged his beer and nodded with satisfaction, like he'd known all along the answers to these questions.

"We're not those men you know from the titty clubs," Sal said. "I don't need to go out to look for a good time. I don't feel like I have to go hunt and be on the prowl."

Tammy didn't say anything. Her squinched-up eyes had taken on the panic of a startled, trapped animal.

Sal leaned down so that his gaze was level with hers. "You know why? Why I don't have to go hunt and be on the prowl, be no caged tiger on the loose or whatever you want to call it?"

Tammy shook her head.

"'Cause I got my pussy at home, that's why. And let me tell you. It is some damn good pussy."

"God-*damn*, boy!" Pete said.

The two men knocked beers like high fives. Pete's whoop rang mocking over all the other drunks in the room, over the sounds of the bartenders behind the bar yelling at each other, over Lenore's own face burning hot in humiliation for Tammy. When Lenore looked at her, she was sorry. What was left of Tammy was done in, crushed. Like a flattened aluminum can. A leopard-print skin hanging off scathed flesh and bone.

Just someone's mommy who'd been cooped up for too long.

It was well after two in the morning when nine women made their way back to Melissa Goldman's house. Jackie wanted to know if there was a bathroom close by. "I have to pee! You didn't tell me we'd be walking so far!"

"It's not that far," Jinx told her. "We're only a block away."

"Oh, I'm with Jackie," Tammy said. "I gotta pee bad."

"I don't know about you, but I feel fabulous!" Melissa stopped walking and stood in the middle of the dark street. "You hear that, everyone? *Fabulous*!"

"Smashing!" Camilla agreed. She walked listing slightly to the left, as if one leg was longer than the other. She was by far the drunkest of them all.

In just a few days, Camilla would vow to spend the rest of her life with one man.

Watching Camilla weave back and forth across the road, Lenore felt slightly seasick. The top of her skull throbbed. All that noise, all that beer. All that noise. It was like repetitive blows to her head. Smashing.

She contemplated the possibility that, tonight while she was gone, Duane might have called for her. What if she'd been home?

Did it matter?

Full bladder or not, Tammy was still the caged tiger on the loose. She would be all right. The female was the more powerful of the species.

"RrrrRRRRR!" she growled, and clawed at an imaginary victim in the air. "Where is my man?"

In the cool night of Cocoa Beach, Lenore shuddered.

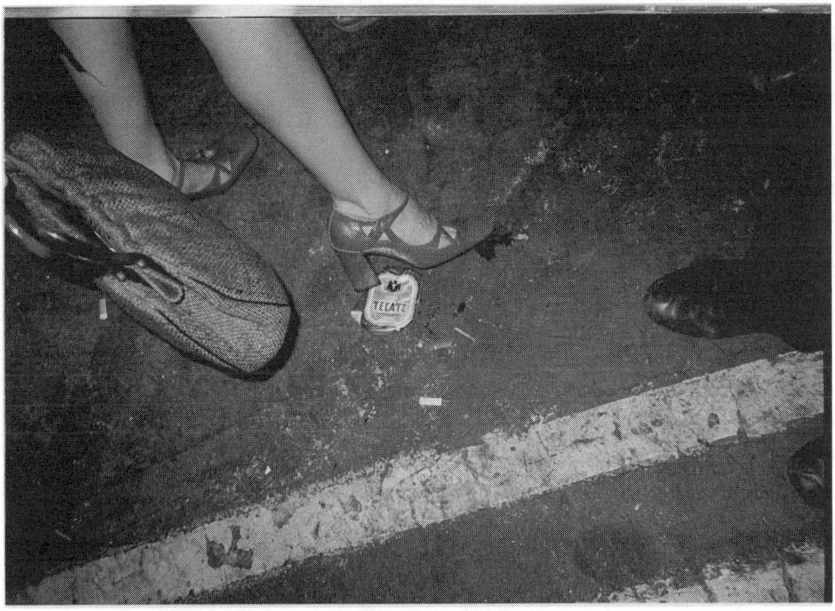
TECATE

# Idle Sketches

Seth Swaaley

Nine in the morning, looking out the window of my room in Lisbon, Portugal. Down below the street's alive with the ongoing storm of A.M. movement. Wrinkled men and women sell lottery tickets. Shoe shiners sit idle on boxed corners drinking tall cans of beer. The café patios are full of tourists and locals eating pastries, drinking espressos, discussing the weather. Thousands of pigeons collectively shit on a statue across the street. Taxicabs and scooters zoom up and down Rua Aurea like horses just out of the gates. In the distance sits a six-hundred-year-old castle. The sun cuts through the clouds like razor madness. The soothing orchestra of foreign music dances across the yellow walls. Eyes close... sinking into the depths of unfamiliar dreams…

* * *

Dark-skinned couples with thousand-year-old blood walk down the street hand in hand. There's an African man with bulging eyes—the whites all red—selling cheap jewelry. The Moroccan hash dealers with the black hair greased back smile and flash their gold teeth and say under their breath, "Hashish?" Old men with big bellies and chest hair foaming from their half-buttoned shirts stand against a brick wall smoking cigars, smiling, yelling at one another. I understand one word out of every twenty. I'm relegated to that frustrating world of dementia that lies somewhere between the ears.

"Say, Pablo, how's the wife?"

"Oh, she's fine Fernando, just fine. Can I get another one of those cigars?"

"Sure. So, is the shop keeping you busy?"

"Yeah, five percent increase in sales this year. At this rate Isabella and I will be able to retire in five years."

Laughter… smoke… cobblestones... red wine. The moon goes down like a shot of crazed light. It's the imagination that keeps us going. Without it, I would've slit the wrists years ago.

* * *

A bar in Seville, three in the afternoon. A man in his middle thirties, German born, married and living in Spain for the last ten years, explains the Sevillen woman to me:

"My friend, nowhere in Spain are there more beautiful women than here in Seville. In Madrid, they're all dirty. In the north, they talk strange. To win over the Sevillan women is a true work of art. You see, my friend, the woman is like the bull, the man is like the matador."

The German puts a pointed index finger from each hand down on the wooden bar. One finger represents the bull, the other the matador. They proceed to dance around one another. Finger puppetry at its finest.

"Here is the matador. He circles around the bull. The bull retreats. The matador moves in again. The bull steps back. It's the timing. One day, the bull gives the matador the look. It's all in the eyes of the bull. The matador makes his final move toward the bull. This time the bull doesn't move. *This*, my friend, is how a man gets a hold of a Sevillan woman."

* * *

Walking the narrow sidewalks of Madrid aimlessly, running upstream in the hoards of humanity. Twelve-year-old kids drink fifths of whiskey in parks till four A.M. I curiously watch it all. The young Moroccans—they're not quite to the gold-teeth stage—unload their drugs and flash the white powder and say to me, "Make you see God." McDonald's, Burger King, Subway, they've all made their mark; fuckin' American capitalism at its best.

The only women who talk to me are the fat hookers in the Chueca district. "Muy guapo," they say as I walk by. Last night I stumbled upon some silver painted drag queens on stilts wearing helmets with horns, some big outdoor dance party. Spent a day at the museums. The Picassos and Goyas kept me entertained, but once you've seen a hundred Jesus and Marys, all the paintings start to look the same.

* * *

Sick of the tourist cities so I take a bus to a small, out of the way town called Palencia. Followed the first pension sign I saw. I walk up four flights of stairs and knock on the door. A short, plump, Spanish woman with a face full of electricity stands in front of me. She sees the dark hair and the black jeans and is convinced I'm Spanish. My poor ability to converse tells her otherwise. She laughs and shows me her plaques and framed certificates from when she worked as a maid for various Swedish and German royalty. Well, at least that's what I think she's saying, but who knows. I'm just about to walk into my room when I'm overwhelmed by the sweet aroma of tomato sauce and sausage.

"Smells good," I say in my half-ass Spanish.

"Quieres?" Maria asks.

"Cuanto cuesto?"

"Nada."

Maria grabs a hold of my hand and drags me into the kitchen and hands me an overflowing plate of noodles, sauce, chorizo, and bread. I dig in. Maria watches me eat and smiles.

"Bueno, si?"

"Oh, yeah, Maria, this is great."

"Te gusta vino?" she asks. Maria goes into a lengthy description of the wine. This isn't the cheap stuff. This is good wine. Aged in the vineyards of Castillan valleys. You can't drink it fast; you've got to sip it.

A rickety, bald-headed man walks into the kitchen. His name's Antonio. He lives in a room on the fifth floor. Maria says he's "loco." Antonio grabs a bottle of wine and pours himself a tall glass and sits down at the table.

Maria shows me a picture of her daughter. She's a flamenco singer. She'll be traveling with a group in September, throughout Spain, Portugal, and France. Suddenly, Maria begins to serenade me in a deep voice full of vibrato. Looking at her I get the feeling I'm in the presence of a beneficent angel. "The man takes one step forward, the woman takes one step back, the man brings out the wine, the woman…" Shit, the German was right. I raise my glass and dance around the room; some sort of Russian jig is all I can come up with. Antonio cracks his bones and joins in. He spins in circles. Maria fills my glass and together we yell, "*Salud*!" The kitchen is alive with music and laughter. This is the life.

* * *

The plan was to go to Braganca, a barren and unmodernized region of Northeast Portugal, but somehow I misread the bus schedule. There's no way to get across the border unless I wait in this small, industrial town for another week. I opt for a train that's headed through the northwest of Spain.

After five hours, I get off in a city called Oriense. I know nothing about the place, but it's big enough that it shouldn't be hard to find a cheap room. The city looks a lot like Pittsburgh; most of the houses and apartments are built on hills; a big river divides the city into separate quadrants. I'm not up for observations, though. I'm tired. I'm hung over. I just want to eat and sleep. The month of non-stop traveling and drinking is beginning to wear on me.

I get a sandwich at a bar and walk back towards my hotel room. On the way, I notice well over a couple thousand people congregating at a park. Families are drinking, middle-aged men are playing soccer, children are running around. I stand against a fence and watch it all, the fuckin' outsider.

From the corner of my eye I notice a black man. Normally, this wouldn't catch my attention, but since I've seen very few black people in the last week, I turn around curiously. On a wall behind me are large posters of James Brown. Hold on, I'm probably seeing things. I take a closer look.

*James Brown*
*August 6*
*Esta Noche a la Ocho*
*1500 Pesetas*

I can't believe it! James Brown! The Godfather of Soul! The Sex Machine! In the middle of nowhere Spain! Tonight! What are the odds? I feel a newborn jolt of life shoot through the veins. It's too hard to hold in my excitement. I grab a hold of the guy standing next to me and say, "James Brown, esta noche, aquí?"

"Si," he says, uninterested.

I run over to the ticket booth. A whole nine American dollars to witness the Funky Chicken. I follow the line of people and end up in a dirt soccer field. It seems like the entire town is here. Old women hang out of their balcony windows. The sky goes dark, a full moon sits straight above, the smell of hash permeates every five feet. A spotlight focuses on the center of the stage. An announcer comes on the microphone. He introduces the members of the band. And then *he* walks out. The man. The myth. The legend.

The Spanish crowd erupts into a sea of chanting: "Jamesa Browna! Jamesa Browna!" I join in, laughing hysterically. The funk kicks in. "Baby, baby, baaaby... baby, baby, baaaby... I got the feelin'." Spanish mothers do a dance that resembles the twist. Arms wave. More hash. My hips and shoulders start to go on their own. After the first song, I scream, "The Payback!" The crowd goes wild: "Jamesa Browna! Jamesa Browna!"

So it's not exactly the same James Brown I've always envisioned. He's a step slow. His face is pretty torn up. The voice is almost shot. He sings about half of the parts, the saxophone and horn sections solo over what were once vocals. But hell, the man has to be eighty. He can still move the feet, though. He hasn't lost the microphone stand tricks, the clench-fisted-kneel-downs, the six different colored flashy jackets, the twenty-year-old big-breasted supermodels in his arms. And sure, maybe the fact that he's only playing for nine bucks in Spain says something about his current financial situation, but I don't care. I'm loving every minute of it.

* * *

A blistering Porto sun shines light across the faces of fully dressed girls and boys as they jump into the Rio Douro and the old women break their black-dressed bones over cobblestones and there's a bar up the hill with wooden swinging doors where the men are covered in tattoos and sit on boxes and play checkers and a glass of wine is a quarter and across the river the gondolas carry the barrels of port to the Atlantic and I'm dangling my legs over a wall and raising my half-empty bottle straight into the eyes of a sunset full of laughing suicide and dreaming of someone to hold and finding myself in a place where time is nothing more than a tired joke.

* * *

Back in Lisbon, sitting outside of a small cerveceria, drinking countless beers in the shade, chewing on a meat pie of some sort. My plane leaves tomorrow. Hard to believe this is it. The last five weeks feel like a blur. Not looking forward to the senseless routine that awaits back home. Guess there's no point in worrying about it now.

Across from me sits a crazy Frenchman named Daniel. He's dressed in tie-dye blue jeans that are rolled up around his ankles, white high tops, a short-sleeved flannel, and has a hairstyle that is on the verge of entering mullet status. I suppose fashion-wise, he never quite escaped the eighties. He lives on a small, French colonized island an hour off the Canadian coast. Works for a local television station. Leads a pretty straight life when he's back home, but when he goes on vacation, anything's fair game. Right now he's on the lookout for hash.

Daniel signals one of the Moroccans over. I've found myself weary of these guys ever since the first day I stepped off of the plane. They seem like the type who can give you a sincere smile one second, and then have a knife shooting through your gut the next. Daniel leaves with one of the Moroccans and tells me he'll be back in a few minutes.

A half an hour later Daniel comes back. He pulls a crumpled cigarette pack and some rolling papers out of his pocket and places them on the table. "Fifty bucks for a gram, I don't know, this better be some good shit."

He reaches for what he thinks is a bar of hash out of the pack. I glance down and notice a small chip of wood. Besides that, the rest of the pack is empty. Beer nearly shoots out of my nose as I try to hold in the laughter. Daniel's face turns red. He breaks the piece of wood.

"That son of a beech, that fuckin' son of a beech! I'm going to get a knife and kill that son of a beech!"

"Shit, man, I'm sorry."

"Wud' dee fuck. I can't believe it. In all my life, all my travels, this never happens, and now today, that son of a beech!"

"You didn't check it when you gave him the money?"

"No, he handed it to me quick. There was a cop close by. I just stuck it in my pocket."

After about ten minutes of cursing in French and English and some other language I can't decipher, Daniel finally joins in my fit of laughter. I'm really trying to stop, but I can't help it.

"Damn, Daniel, I'm sorry, a piece of wood? I've never seen that one before."

"I know, he got me," he says, smiling.

Daniel has a perverted comment for every woman who walks by. "Great ass." "Look at those tits." "I need to fuck." He tells me about the time that he paid five bucks to have sex with a fifteen-year-old prostitute in Cuba. She took him up to a room while her boyfriend stood outside and waited. He felt a little strange about it, being that he was twice her age, but he says shamelessly, she was one of the best fucks he's ever had. Behind the beer, I wrestle with that disturbing thought.

We roam around the city for hours, every now and then stopping in a bar to escape the blazing heat. At dinner Daniel spends the entire time trying to educate me on the differences between good and bad wine, the proper way to hold the glass, whether the wine bleeds down the sides of the glass, how important a good cheese is in bringing out the flavor, blah, blah. It's a bit boring, yet at the same time comical to listen to.

It's after midnight on Sunday and the streets are dark and empty. My flight leaves at seven in the morning. I'm ready to call it a night. Daniel says I can't go to sleep now, I'll never wake up in time. He wants to at least buy me one last drink.

We walk into a bar on one of the side streets of the Baixa district. Besides a small group of teenagers sitting at a table in the far corner, the bar's pretty empty. Daniel keeps looking behind him. There's an attractive woman who looks to be in her forties, sitting alone at a table.

"I don't know about that woman," says Daniel. "She's just in here drinking by herself. Maybe she wants to fuck."

"Well, go talk to her then," I say, leaving him at the bar and finding a table in the other room. How the hell did I end up with this guy? A couple of minutes later, Daniel and the woman come over and sit down. The woman doesn't speak English and Daniel speaks Portuguese so I'm pretty much out of the conversation. Understanding a few words in between, I find out that the woman is recently divorced and a Fado dance instructor. After that it's all foreign music. Daniel buys her a drink. He's trying to convince her to come home with him. He whispers something in her ear. She laughs, but it's not one of those you're-charming laughs; it's the you're-a-fool laugh. The woman gets up from the table and goes to the bathroom. I tell Daniel I don't think anything's going to happen. He keeps at it. An hour later the woman leaves, despite the pleas of Daniel. He sits at the table putting down the rum and coke, a pathetic portrait of dejection. He slams the drink down. "Ugh, I need to fuck. Let's get out of here."

Daniel's screaming his sexual frustrations into the night. He's driving me crazy. It's too much to handle. I tell him I know of a place. Some New Zealander pointed it out to me a couple of nights ago. I'm not sure if it's open this late, being Sunday and all, but I'll show him where it is. Suddenly, his eyes light up.

"How much?"

"I don't know. You'll have to handle that," I say.

I take Daniel down a twisting maze of back streets and dark alleys. A few stray cats follow us for a couple blocks. In the distance you can hear the late-night echo of street cleaners. Finally, we stop at a door with a red curtain.

"You sure this is it?" asks Daniel.

"Yeah, I think so. I hear music in there."

A young woman walks up behind us. She's got a sad face covered in acne scars and is wearing tight black vinyl pants that struggle to hold in the curves of her body.

"Make love?" she asks Daniel.

"Yeah, how much?" he says, bluntly.

"10,000 Escudos."

"In there?" he asks, pointing towards the red curtain.

"Yes," she says, "follow me."

Daniel looks at me with a grin on his face. "Well, I guess this is it."

"Yeah, Daniel, it's been fun. Good luck with the rest of your trip. Enjoy the night."

Daniel and the woman disappear behind the curtain. I'm left standing alone in the middle of the street, lighting up a smoke, talking to the moon, knowing that tomorrow this whole entire trip will just seem like some strange, mystic dream.

* * *

Six hour daze. Ears decompressing. The Manhattan skyline comes into view. A Portuguese college girl who's visiting America for the first time looks over my shoulder.

"Is that it?" she asks.

"Yup, that's New York."

"Wow."

Her eyes are big and black and beautiful. I give her my window seat. It wasn't that long ago that I had that same sense of wonder and excitement. I suppose it only comes in doses, but damn, it sure is a nice feeling to have.

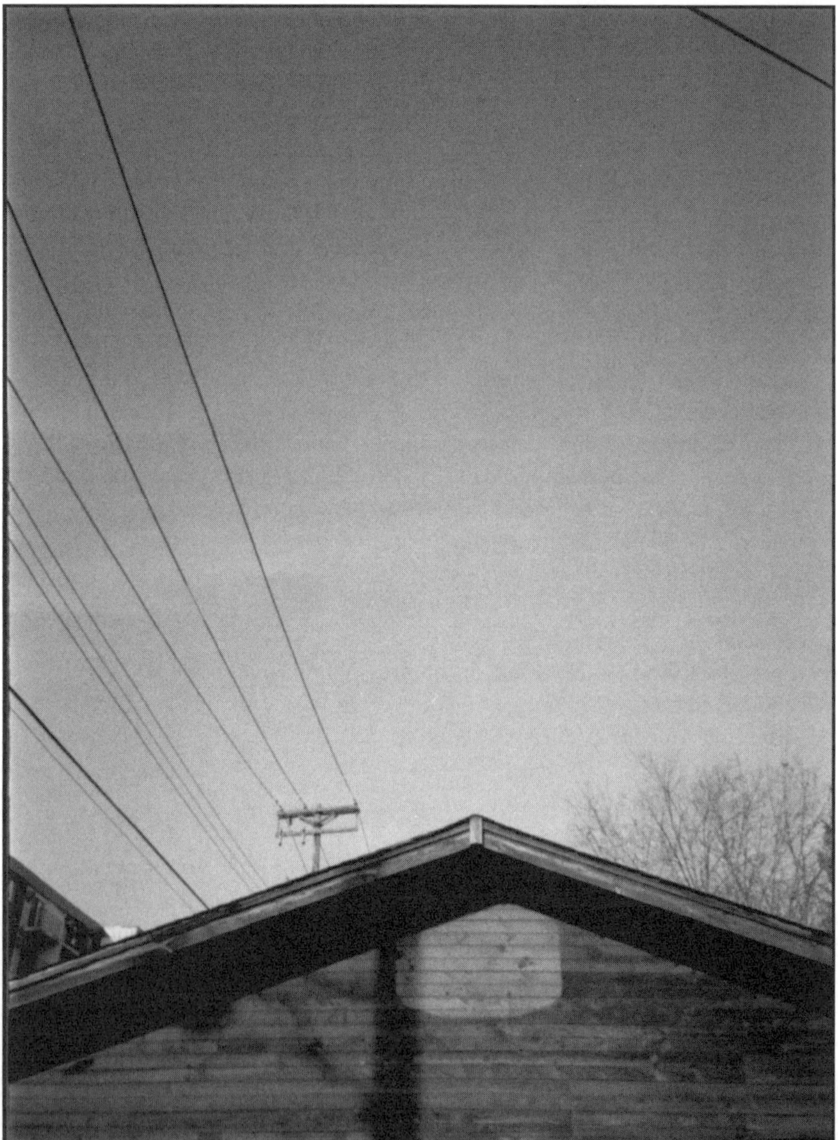

# Marauders

Jerry Gabriel

We traveled like gypsies to these little towns—places called Mudsock and Comersville and just plain Water. We set up our camps and cooked hot dogs on fires started inconspicuously in a corner of the parking lot, or back in a small wood where some unnamed brook ran. These were tournaments, mostly, and we planned on staying for the duration. We knew that the Marauders would be involved in whatever it was that happened last. We knew that we would walk away with the biggest trophy and that we would sit in the Shamrock later and revel in the victory. We congregated in the bleachers and donned maroon and gold clothing. We knitted hats and gloves of these colors for our children and grandparents. We smoked under the empty skies at night, at half-time, say, when you could see all the way to the next galaxy and the cold made you giddy with its bite. We drank in the parking lot afterwards, straight from the bottle—cheap wines and low-end whiskey. We embraced each other and gave high fives. We drove recklessly through the hills and honked our horns to the darkness.

We followed the Marauders that winter with fervor, purpose. We cheered them on, bloodthirsty, calling, like ancient Romans, for the annihilation of their opponents. A few of our number had been there in other seasons—in the days when the Marauders struggled to win half their games—but only a few. Graham Wilson, the old World War II vet, who sat in bibbed overalls and chewed on Swisher Sweet cigars, he had been one of them. He had followed them for decades—into every dinky one-horse town in southeast Ohio, every backwater gym where five opposing boys and at least one ref could be scrounged up. He'd tell stories about it at the Shamrock late at night, when everyone had returned from a game and was sitting victoriously with a Genesee in hand. He told of less talented teams, of boys we knew—some of whom were now of our number—boys who as men would work for the county road crew or the tile plant or Goodyear. He told of crooked referees, hostile crowds, buzzer-beating jumpers. Heartbreak was always somehow inherent. And our hearts were broken anew each time. We loved to listen because even if we hadn't been there through it all, they felt like our stories too.

And one of those stories was in the making one cold February night, right in the heart of winter, when darkness comes on too early and stays too late. We shuffled ourselves from our corps of minivans and Dodge Colts that night, the vinyl seats cracking under us from the cold. We slapped each other on the back, traded jocular insults. We smoked one last cigarette and then descended the stairs into this CCC-constructed elementary, ducking so as not to hit our heads on the low-hanging, asbestos-covered pipes.

We came out on a long, dark hallway, and it seemed improbable that this was even a school; it seemed more a hospital or a factory's dank basement. But the high-pitched noise of new sneakers stopping on a polished floor drifted toward us from the far end of the hall. There were voices, too, the low murmur of strip-miners and backhoe operators and soy farmers. We moved in that direction, cautiously. And when we turned a corner to find ourselves in the gymnasium, we all felt the excitement that we by then expected. It went, like they say, straight down the spine, and spread outward from there until your entire body felt high. It was a feeling we lived for.

Great caged phosphorous bulbs lit the gym from above, and we saw immediately, in two neat lines beginning at half-court, our Marauders, in the middle of one of their elaborate warm-up drills. At the other end of the court was a group of ragamuffin boys clad in unwashed and unmatching jerseys. One of them wore a pair of work boots with no socks and had a head of hair in bad need of a brushing. We glanced at one another, suppressing laughs, though something here felt sad, too.

So many of us had fallen into our lives in the days and weeks and years leading up to that time—deep into an abysmal rut of small-town receptionist by day and movie renter by night. It was monotony. We were beaten down, really, and gaining weight in unproud ways. We lived off Tommy's Pizza and Yankee Burger, Milwaukee's Best, strawberry daiquiris. We talked, before this, only of the time we'd been to Virginia Beach and Gatlinburg, though we never even considered the idea of going again; it seemed somehow impossible. It was always, *Remember that little restaurant we found down on that side street near the water? The Outrigger, was it? Pirate Jack's?* And, the reply: *My God, did they have good deep-fried shrimp.* A confirming nod, a wistful look, a whispered *Damn.*

And the Marauders, with their shiny maroon and gold uniforms, these handsome young boys on the verge of life, their snappy warm-up drills, their hustle—they pulled us out of it; we all readily admitted that these boys had saved us. We were convinced that we would have followed them to the end of the earth. That is what they came to mean to us.

Their parents we treated as royalty. We were so thankful for them having brought these beautiful guardian angels into the world that we bought them hot pretzels and coffees. We made them macramé and quilts and gave them badges with their sons' pictures on them. We bought their gas and gave them the best motel rooms when we were down on a long trip, down into West Virginia. These people were saints to us. We loved them as we loved their children.

The Marauders were undefeated that February—25-0—and there was no one, we were sure, who could beat them. Unquestionably it was the Year of the Marauders.

Certainly they'd had good years before. Walter Haskins, who was the press operator at the *Daily Messenger*, had made a scrapbook of their history—clippings he'd dug out of the paper's archives. He showed it around sometimes at games, in lulls in the play, or in someone's van on the road to an out-of-the-way tournament. The *Messenger* had always followed the Marauders because their coach, Sam Paris, was the sports editor there. He had written all twenty-five years of Marauder history himself. And we enjoyed looking at the photos of these boys who were now men, reading about the limits of their accomplishments. The more limited the past, we somehow reasoned, the more promising the future.

We had become part of the Marauders early that season, on a whim. One day sitting around the Shamrock, someone said we should go down to Winslow to see these boys play. There was some grousing, but we weren't doing anything else to speak of, and so we piled into cars and drove the hour to see them put a good beating on these Winslow boys. Afterwards, we were hooked. We had been sleepwalking through our lives at the County Ag. Extension Agency, the Falls Boot Shop, the Bottleneck Paper Mill, and the Marauders shook us.

That night, we drove all the way to Parkersburg on our way home to find an open bar where we could celebrate. Later, we even took to going to some of their practices at the old Central Furnace Elementary gym; we cheered them even there, during their drills.

In retrospect, our expectations might have been unfair—to us, to them—but then there is finally no fairness in such matters. We needed them and they appeared, winners, riding a streak, gathering trophies. No one doubted that we would walk into Columbus in March and sweep the state tournament. There was talk of an AAU National Tournament berth, a trip to Atlanta.

And so, when, that overcast Friday evening in February, we found ourselves in yet another insubstantial hamlet somewhere in the hinterlands of Grover County, Ohio, trailing at the beginning of the second period by eleven points to a group of kids who looked more like peasants from some forgotten epoch than a basketball team, we panicked. When that lead began to grow to proportions we'd never before been on the receiving end of, our panic became tangible.

Coach Sam Paris was a second-rate newspaperman, we all agreed, but he had a way of sapping every ounce of potential out of his teams. And this team's potential, we were given to understand, was unparalleled. Their leader was a boy named C.R. Conner, who was actually thirteen and had to use a fake birth certificate, which Haskins had created himself in the *Messenger*'s pressroom. Even in sixth grade, Conner had been mentioned in a small piece in *Street and Smith* as an upcoming and promising college prospect, and there had been on occasion coaches from far-off cities to the north snooping around Marauder games, trying to get a look at this wonder.

When he scored, which, most nights, he did a lot, we whooped and hollered. We carried on. We couldn't help but express our joy in wild gyrations and raised fists. Conner was a forward and played with the poise of someone, we figured, twice his age. He moved so gracefully, slicing through opposing defenses for scores: reverse lay-ups, turnaround jumpers. "There's a certain number of things you can teach a kid," someone once observed of Conner, "and after that, it's all instincts. Either the kid's got 'em or he don't."

C.R. Conner had good instincts in aces. The other boys looked to him for leadership and inspiration, and he just about never let them down.

Except that night, in this town—there was some argument about whether it was called Riverton or Woodville—he faltered. He looked tired, like he hadn't slept, and we—shamefully; there are no excuses to be offered now—we suggested a number of unjust possibilities for this—among them: drugs, a pregnant girlfriend, more failed classes.

We were at the height of our powers then. None of us had ever known such invincibility. People at work or at the mall in Sugarton or even at the grocery store—they seemed to notice this new confidence, and many of them even said as much. We enjoyed going to the bowling alley on an off night and bowling a few games; we all had personal bests that season. But we grew boisterous and arrogant, ridiculing folks on other lanes, calling over to the bar to have our beers brought to us. We talked loudly and wore loud clothes, funny hats. And we drank enormous amounts and woke up the next morning unfazed, like the nineteen-year-olds we no longer were.

With the Marauders down, though, we felt the wind knocked from us. It wasn't something we could prepare for. This game was meant to be but a warm-up for a large tournament in Kentucky the next week. It was a practice, really, and one that we all, regrettably, looked past.

At first, we cheered louder. We tongue-lashed the referees to call a fair game, which in our estimation they were not doing. But these boys—we'll call them the Rockets, though they might have been the Green Dragons or the Flying Tigers or any number of other things—they had come to play and were putting it on our Marauders: they, in their hand-me-down Converse; they, in their elementary cafeteria/gym, its floor sticky from spilled Jell-O, its walls covered in the grotesque art of Valentine's Day hearts and cupids; they, the downtrodden of the downtrodden, were defeating our undefeated, invincible Marauders. And with Coach Paris, whose play-calling we also questioned for a time, we grew apoplectic.

Paris called time-outs and we could hear his seething voice berating our boys. We could hear, in the imposed quiet, the scuff of chalk on chalkboard. We saw the faces of the boys, and their fear was great. We heard their lungs gasping for air, like men emerged from the depths. The weight of our civilization along the banks of the Falls River was on their shoulders somehow, and they were surely all too aware of this fact—at least we were.

As soon as we fell behind, some of the weaker of our number—Mrs. Hollins, for one—decided not to watch. She went to her car where, she later admitted, she found a distant university's classical radio station to which she could ride out the loss. She said she thought about the garden she would plant that spring, creating vast mental lists of all that she would put in it, the variations of potatoes and beans and squash, and all the ways she would care for those things. Inside, we ate candy bars and drank flat soda and some of us prayed, but the lead grew inordinately. Our boys were alienated on the court, hesitant. They seemed such little children.

Paris's assistant, Michael Watson, a sixth grade science teacher at Hilltop Elementary, talked to Paris, entreated him. He would observe the court and then scribble maniacally on the chalkboard and show it to Paris, but Paris would look away; he seemed inconsolable.

Paris himself had been the sixth man on Falls High's only championship team of the last thirty years, and a few remembered him as the unskilled kid who came in to make life miserable for an opposing guard. He was prone to starting fights, one man remembered, though some of the other old-timers believed that the coach of that time had put him up to many of those fights, had sicced him on an opposing star in order to get them both ejected.

Paris, though, was no stranger to defeat, just as he was no stranger to victory. Though many of us had looked judgmentally upon his poor writing for years, we had all gained a great deal of respect for him as a coach, and when Carla Randolph began to assert that this was his fault—and many of us tried on that idea, too—one of the true followers—it may have been Graham Wilson himself, who had fought off the Germans one yard at a time at the Bulge, turned to a group of us and said, "Just look at y'all. Y'all make me ashamed to be a Marauder." And then we were all ashamed too, to the bones.

At half time with the Marauders down by 24, some of us went to look for a bar in the little village—just a little shot in the arm to bolster ourselves, we said. On our way out, we passed the cafeteria kitchen that the Marauders were using as a locker room. The door was ajar and we could see that Paris was in the face of C.R. Conner, spit spraying from his mouth as he tore into the boy. The other boys sat impassively beyond them, exchanging water bottles. Some of them sat with their hands splayed on their bowed heads like young men who had just lost wives in a natural disaster.

* * *

Dim and dusty neon signs offered Bud and Miller Lite through the single, television-sized window outside the tavern we found. It was bitter cold that night, below zero, and we shuffled through the interminable flurries and the sand parking lot frozen solid. There were four trucks parked in the lot with provocative bumper stickers. One said that "Coonhunters Do It All Night Long" and another asserted the inferiority of some Middle Eastern nation. It was not the Shamrock, but we needed direly to regroup, to get a handle on what was happening. Inside, the locals leered at us from their bar stools. They played pinball on dirty machines that looked old enough to have been the first ones that country had ever seen.

As we sipped at our first drinks, Turner Olson suggested that perhaps the game was fixed. Hell no, we said. Impossible. We speculated on such theories as the full moon and the re-emergence of

Paris's ex-wife in Falls the week prior. But we couldn't get our finger on the situation. None of it seemed to add up.

We ordered a second round. Someone said that we should be getting back, but none us made a move toward the door. Soon, Terry Winston was telling stories about his days as a Marauder, fifteen or twenty years ago, and we listened intently.

"Paris was tough," Winston was saying. "A mean streak a mile long." His eyes lit up as he tried to retrieve that past so far behind him now. He talked of a time when his knees were good and of a game he once scored 21 points in.

We were transfixed, listening like second graders to his tales. He told story after story, about this boy or that—we knew them all—about Paris, his coaching strategies. One anecdote involved Paris, a boy named Chuck Wolf, and a full water bottle Paris had thrown across a gymnasium at the boy.

"It flew," Winston said, "right over his head and through one of the stained glass windows of this Catholic school's gym over in Chillicothe."

We all laughed at the image of Paris throwing a bottle at this boy, and then there was a quiet when our laughs trailed off. Terry Winston shook his head.

"He'd scream bloody murder at us," he said. "Every minute of every game. He threatened us and insulted our manhood, ridiculed us." He looked up to all of us sitting there at the table.

"We never won a game," he said. "We did not win one game. Not ever." Mindy Hagan put her arm around him. He lowered his head and raised it again.

"But he would come into the locker room afterwards and he would tell us how proud he was of us, and that he thanked God for us."

Winston was on the verge of tears when Tad Phillips thought to order a bratwurst from the rotisserie from behind the bar, and the moment was averted. We all remembered then that we hadn't eaten and we all ordered bratwursts and more beers and there was a general clatter as these things were delivered to us and as we paid for them. Every one of us must have had a moment of realization around then when it was clear what sort of people we were. We were not what any of us wanted to be, and after a while it sunk in that we could not go back to that gym and show our pitiful faces there.

This caused us to drink more and, hours later, when there was not a soul left in this tiny bend in the road save its official residents and three carloads of lost Fallians, we stumbled to our cars and drove off into the cold of a winter night, our futures once again dried up.

We passed the aging elementary school on our way out of town. It was lit by one dim yellow security bulb burning at a lonesome corner, the void of its parking lot obliquely illuminated. We were silent as we slipped back into the forests of that country, the winding roads, the nothing that that place sometimes is. We checked our Rand McNally for the way home, and after several wrong turns and desolate stretches of emptiness, we made our way back into Falls County and then into Falls proper. It was two in the morning then, and we drove past the Shamrock, which was dark and closed, and we were all thankful not to face the choice of going in. We went home to our various residences, to the quiet and defeat of the lives we hoped we had escaped. Those lives, of course, were still there waiting for us, just as we'd left them months before, and we all felt them slip back toward us that night as we lay awake and waited for dawn.

* * *

When dawn finally did come, it was barely recognizable, overcast and filled with more flurries and cold and wind like we rarely experienced in those hills. When the paper came out that afternoon and confirmed the rumor that had been circulating around town all morning—that the Marauders had won the night previous in a come-from-behind victory—many of us were at the Shamrock, hiding in coves in the back, eating fish sandwiches.

We were wordless, most of us. A few tried to dig up the old enthusiasm, saying that the folks down in Moorehead, Kentucky better get ready, that the Marauders were going to storm the place. But this convinced no one, and we sat there quietly in long stretches.

And then a curious thing happened: Graham Wilson walked in with a small entourage behind him, men and women we'd known our whole lives, but who just then seemed unrecognizable, as foreign as a carload of Ukranians walking into that bar.

Wilson had an artificial leg—the old heavy kind made of some wood—and he walked with a wiry old cherry cane that seemed such a perfect symbol of his own dogged perseverance in the world. He left his group and came over to ours. Wilson was decades older than us—many decades, in some cases—and we all knew he understood things that we were very far from understanding. He approached our table and looked at us for a long minute without saying anything. He breathed heavily and pulled the unlit cigar from his mouth. We waited, preparing to take on the truth of his words.

"Well," he started. We knew we were in for it.

But it didn't come. He shook his head, and not in a way that disgraced. He said, "I reckon them boys we played last night took it hard. I near felt bad for 'em."

We waited. He looked around the room like there might be a cue out there in the smoky place for what to say to us. He might have said, "You people are pathetic," and he would have been right, or, "You people are as no account as any I've come across." But he said no such thing. What he said was so much harder to take. He said, "We'll need you all down in Ken-tuck next week. We'll need ever last one of youns." And then he limped over to the bar and ordered a brandy and a Genesee.

We sat there, rattled. Nobody spoke for the longest time. There was just the noise of glasses being raised to mouths, of dried fish being chewed.

The wind outside howled against the ancient building, and we sat on the edge of our seats, all seemingly waiting for something inside to snap. Lifetimes of experience told us to go one way, while everything else said to go the other.

We sat without words, and fought in ourselves and, finally, we disbanded. We slid from our seats and paid our tabs and said quiet good-byes and then every one of us walked through the oak door that led to the world outside. We pulled our collars up and we put on our mittens and hats, and we bolstered ourselves against that winter afternoon, and then we walked right into it, some of us without sound, some of us mumbling things to ourselves, and a few of us with clenched fists and our voices crying out—part request, part demand—to the town of Falls or the heavens or some unnamable thing inside. Indecipherable, guttural noises, grunts of the inarticulate, the sound of that part of us that already knew how we would answer the question.

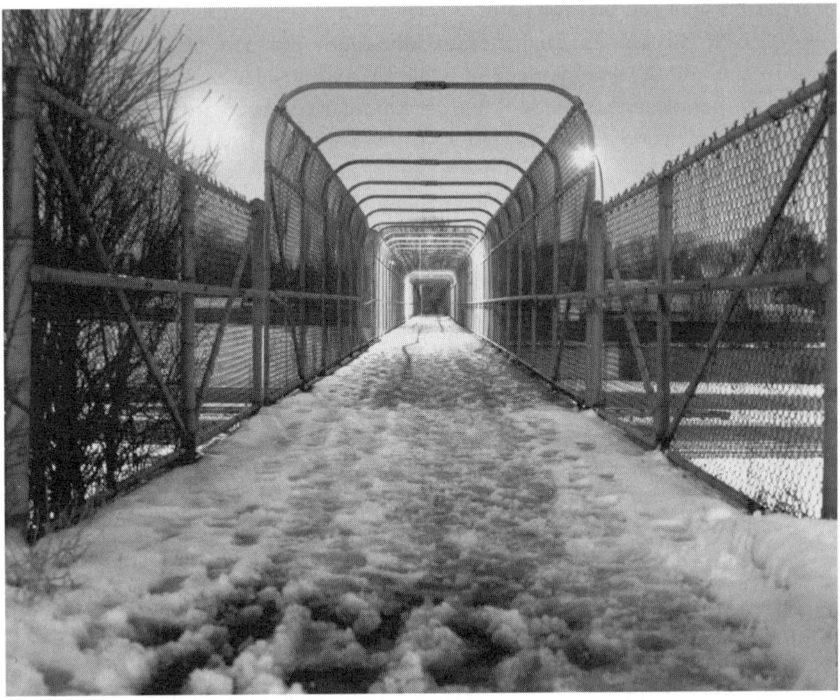

# 23 Bay 23 Bay 23 Bay

Jim Munroe

All I was in for, originally, was the Lost Subway Station. *That* I wanted to see. It appealed to me as a kind of urban Atlantis, disappearing beneath our consciousness and leaving a dizzying swirl of rumor and mystery in its wake. Well, that's a little romantic, but how many hard headed rationalists would be tromping through a grimy tunnel in the wee hours of the morning?

"All I hope is that they don't turn off the lights after it closes," Kevin grumbled. He was mad we had waited till the trains stopped. I had hunkered down in the alcove beside the tracks and refused to move until the 1:10 A.M. train had passed. It didn't make sense to risk getting smushed since it was just a case of waiting for half an hour.

Not that any of this made sense, but I had the tendency to temper my irrational acts with careful logic. It bugged the hell out of Kevin.

"Watch out for the third rail," I said, to razz him. In my best teacherly voice, I elucidated: "The Third Rail provides electricity that allows the subway to run—but it delivers quite a zap."

Kevin snorted in the darkness. "Hey, you remember that bird that was always getting zapped to hell off some powerline or some shit?"

"Waa?"

"The *bird*, man, in the educational commercials—okay, here it is."

We had come to a part of the tunnel where we could see the southbound track between the mammoth supports. A change in the light that I at first processed as a visual mistake, suddenly coalesced into headlights. My body seemed intent at forcing as much blood through my heart as was physically possible.

Kevin threw himself against the wall, the light-dark whipping across his body, and I swear I saw him grin.

A train passed on the far track with unnatural shortness.

"Garbage train," Kevin said.

"What are you *smiling* for," I said, breathless and dizzy and light-headed. "You – fucking – maniac?"

"I wasn't smiling," he said, smiling. He stepped down onto the space between the supports and hopped down onto the other side.

I followed, and found myself on a parallel set of tracks. Ahead of us, unlike the level tracks to the right and left, they dipped downwards. "Wow," I mouthed.

The tunnel, if anything, was just as grimy if not more grimy than the others. More a dust-grime than a grease-grime. The spaces between the concrete supports grew further and further apart as we moved on and down. Another garbage train passed by, this time on the tracks we had just left. I shot Kevin a dark look.

"No accounting for danger, eh, Mr. Safety?" he said lightly. "True adventurers—seekers—can't avoid it." Then, almost as a peace offering, he added, "The third rail's live here, too, so watch it."

We were once again in an enclosed tunnel, lit by a chain of lights along the wall. Every so often there was a door marked with a name so bureaucratic that it may as well have been Sanskrit: *East Holdings Vestibule*.

I started to see graffiti along the walls, not your sophisticated hiphop pieces but more your rocker scrawls: Motorhead, Iron Maiden, and the like. It deflated me a little bit—we weren't exactly the first ones through here—but it also made me feel a little safer that we were walking along a beaten path.

My feeling of safety dissipated a little as the cheesy metal band graffiti gave way to more heavy-duty shit. Names I recognized from reading Lovecraft, runes, less dismissable markings. Kevin was walking ahead, silently, his head not noticeably turning to look at the walls—he'd seen it before, I guess. He stopped when he came to the altar, though.

I would have missed it. In the wall of the tunnel, there was a half circle carved out, about eight feet high. Kevin pulled a zippo out of his pocket and leaned down, lighting stubs of candles I didn't realize were there. His movements were smooth and serious and he stood up and watched the flame for a moment. I couldn't crack a joke, which is what every amazed bone in my body wanted to do, so I tore my eyes away from Kevin's shadowed face and looked at the candles myself.

Continuing from the carved alcove was a line that closed the circle. Within the circle was—of course—a pentagram. It looked like it was actually carved into the concrete, but I couldn't imagine how or why.

"What—" was all I was able to stammer out. I wasn't frightened as much as amazed. How cliché! I mean, would the hooded dudes be coming out with the virginal sacrifice now?

"Just something we did as kids," Kevin said as he leaned over to blow out the flames. (I was just glad he didn't extinguish them with his fingers.) "I'm superstitious, I admit it. That's why midnight *would* have been better." He waggled his finger at me as he said it.

I shrugged and looked away, and my eyes fell across a piece of graffiti on the opposite wall. It was a scrawled pentagram with a women's symbol attached, the words SATANIC FEMINISM beneath it.

I laughed, a little nervously, and pointed.

Kevin walked over to it and lifted a foot, smudging it. It had been written in chalk. "There's no respect left in this ironic age," he said in a musing tone, obliterating the chalk scuff by deliberate scuff.

* * *

When I tell people this story, this is the part where they break in with "*Where* did you find this *freak*?!" So I'll assume you're thinking the same thing.

It was on a rooftop a month previous. The highest building on campus, to be specific. I was in the habit, after my Thursday class, of checking the door to the roof. It was just an extra floor up, so I would just go up, check, then go two flights down and take the elevator from there.

And one fine June day it was open.

There is nothing quite like the smooth turn of a usually locked knob. I checked to confirm that it was unlocked on both sides before I let it click closed behind me.

The rooftop was as glorious as I had imagined. A great view of the York University campus below, a terrifically blue sky above, and, straight ahead, a guy striding purposefully towards me.

Shit.

I quelled the primordial fight-flee instinct. Nothing screams *guilty* as loudly as running.

"You're not supposed to be in this area," he said in clipped tones.

"Oh," I said. "The door was unlocked... I guess I went up an extra flight. I have a class on the 25th floor."

"Not bad, not bad..." Kevin said, smiling. "Good eye contact, calm and assured, plausible reason." He stuck out his hand and we did a one-pump that felt like a secret handshake.

I was a dilettante next to him, a dabbler—he'd actually learned to pick locks and was to blame for the rooftop door being open. He wanted an acolyte, someone with the same strange sensibility of wonder and curiosity, someone to buy him beer.

In the bar after a foray into some abandoned wing of a hospital, I welded the friendship with a random observation.

I lifted the fifth mug of draft to my lips and pulled it away, overcoming my self-consciousness. "In a way, the places we're going—they're like these grey husks that bureaucracy sheds. These huge... insect skins."

I could actually see it in his eyes that it made a sudden and complete sense to him. I smiled, giddy with the pleasure of something well said. I had been rolling it around in my head since the second beer, but it took a while to break the sound barrier.

He stood and lifted his beer. "To the insectile husks of the system," he said grandly to the bar at large, and there was a dull roar of approval and clinking.

* * *

So I had followed this guy, who I knew nothing about other than that I had a dim reflection of his obsession, up into the heights of skyscrapers and down into the bowels of the earth.

Now, as we entered the fabled Lower Bay Station, it was a bit of a letdown. The lettering on the wall read CHARON.

"What?" I intoned campily. "Have you led me into the pits of *hell*?" I had to say something to break the weird tension.

"That's from when they were filming a movie down here," he explained. "There's the real lettering." It read BAY, not even LOWER BAY, I was disappointed to see. I had heard whispers of this ghost station for years and wanted it to come complete with hordes of treasure, or at least a secret library. But instead, it was just a dirtier than average station.

"I'm gonna take a look around," I said, and Kevin nodded absently. I almost said I hoped he wouldn't start any black masses when I was away, but I was still too tense to joke around.

There was a big fence on the platform around a storage area. Mostly what was in there were stairs for escalators in various states of disrepair. I wondered how many tax dollars were lost when plans for the route which were to use this station were abandoned. I stared at the underside of an escalator stair for the pure joy of seeing the underside of anything usually upright.

I rounded the storage space and noticed that between the fence and the wall there was a four-foot gap littered with debris. A garage sale painting, a few inexplicable photos—one of a beaming guy behind the wheel of his/a car—not enough artifacts to form any sort of profile of the person who left them. A subway worker (I imagined the proud auto owner in uniform) may have decided to cheer the place up, perhaps. Kevin approached while I savored the mystery.

"Whattaya figure?" I gestured at the photo where it lay.

Kevin picked it up. "Car isn't new. This isn't one of them check-out-me-in-my-new-wheel shots."

"Might be used." I scanned the face for signs of shock. Blue eyes, bristle-balding cut, big-ass grin, no shock. "Doesn't look like a caught-unawares shot, either."

"Whatever," Kevin said, slipping it into his back pocket. "It's an odd souvenir." Kevin used odd as a synonym for good, and I had seen his collection of exploration mementos.

"Got something to show ya," he said, jerking his head in the direction. I followed. He was in the habit of doing that silently in more sensitive areas. Made me feel a little like a horse, but I got over the indignity—where we went usually made up for it.

He pushed through a grey door ("picked it" in answer to my unasked question) and closed it behind us. The darkness lasted just long enough to make me wonder why I get involved with people I hardly know who are into satanic rites—and then the fluorescents noisily sputtered to life.

The room we were in was small but uncluttered—practically empty, really, except for the control board and microphone. The control board was spotted with buttons, which (I was relieved to see) were unmarked. Any marking, I was sure, would be a temptation impossible for Kevin to resist.

We were kindred souls in many ways in regards to urban adventuring. Kevin, however, was far more interactive than I. He had pulled a fire alarm ("I knew it was dead," he almost convinced me, "I just dig how it feels.") and another time—

Kevin right then snapped the control board to life. I opened my mouth to protest, but Kevin lifted a tense finger. With his other hand he adjusted the microphone and I could tell from the echoey metallic scrunching that it was on.

"23 Bay 23 Bay 23 Bay" is what he said, and his soft voice bounced around the room with a slight edge of feedback. Or what I thought he said. He made a clicking sound with his throat and, just when I was waiting for his rendition of Twisted Sister's "We're Not

Gonna Take It," he shut everything down.

I was so scared my stomach was clenching. Kevin stared silently at the board, his hand still touching the mike, and I tried to form words. None of it made sense. Why would he do something so ludicrously dangerous as speak over the system-wide intercom? Why was he standing there so frozen and creepy? Why did he choose to send out a code that meant nothing?

* * *

Kevin had taught me the Toronto Transit Commission's subway codes. I had always wondered what those mysterious messages had meant, and over lunch Kevin told them to me as if passing on some kind of oral tradition.

"Repeat after me: 99 Finch 99 Finch 99 Finch."

I humored him. "99 Finch 99 Finch 99 Finch."

"That means they need a mechanic at Finch station," he said, finally extricating his peanut butter sandwich from the Saran wrap. "506 Kennedy 506 Kennedy 506 Kennedy."

I waited, but finally repeated it. "506 Kennedy 506 Kennedy 506 Kennedy."

"They need a custodial crew at Kennedy."

I nodded. "Huh."

"77 College 77 College 77 College."

"77 College 77 College 77 College."

"A jumper."

"What?"

Kevin had finished his sandwich and was palming his wrap into a ball. "Someone's jumped in front of a train. A suicide."

I rolled my eyes. "Bullshit. How often would they need that?"

"I've heard 77 four times so far. Gives me a chill each time."

"I can't even remember hearing about subway suicides. Your info is wrong, man."

Now Kevin rolled his eyes. "You don't hear about it because the newspapers agree to keep it out. Otherwise, people would do it even more often, just for the publicity."

He tossed the cellophane ball at my forehead. It bounced off and rolled to a stop near the salt shaker.

* * *

Kevin had taught me all the codes he knew, and 23 wasn't one of them.

He let go of the mike and nodded for me to leave the room. I did, hoping we'd be making a quick getaway. Maybe he knew some alternate exit...?

At first, on the platform, I mistook the vibration for shaky legs. But when I paused to wait for Kevin to close the door, I was undeceived.

It couldn't be a response to the call, I thought, not this fast. I could tell that Kevin felt it too, in the slow way he turned around.

His eyes were wide. "It... worked."

I would have run at that point, I like to think, if I could have figured out where to run. But the growing sound came from everywhere, and there were no lights in the tunnel. I was sure that the one I picked would lead to sudden death.

I couldn't bear to look at Kevin. I was sure he'd be grinning, and I'm sure I would have decked him. As it was, I soon had other things to look at.

It was the squeaking that I heard first, then the rumbling. From the blackness of the tunnel burst a series of harnessed rats the size of ponies. Dust and grime covered their coats, and I saw as they loped past us (amazing the detail-observance intense fear can inspire), they blinked constantly with the dust.

I forced my head to look, past the dozen or so pairs of rats, down that bizarre train of giant vermin to its burden. It was a Victorian carriage, wooden but for the giant wheels of pocked stone. The implausible wheels were slowing even as I looked upon them.

The figure holding the reigns was a skeleton. I had a brief moment of hope then—this couldn't be real. It had to be a funhouse horror. Kevin had brought me to an old abandoned amusement park, and this was a projection. The cameras were well hidden, probably near the tracks.

The skeleton stood up, set the reins down and hopped to the platform. It was the click of his foot bones on the ceramic surface that caused me to actually shit my pants.

It was a small squirt, thankfully, but I could feel it there, warm and cradled in by my underwear elastic. I had a moment of gratefulness for my briefs before my terror returned full force.

The skeleton moved without the jerky edge that animatronic technology and frame-by-frame animation had taught me to associate with skeletons. He walked towards us, slowly and with a slight hunch.

"Somebody call for a taxi?" he said. He said it jovially, but I couldn't tell if he was grinning or not.

One of the rats snorted.

Kevin didn't reply until the skeleton was standing right in front of us. "This is a taxi?"

The skeleton's head tilted up a little as he said. "It's a joke, son." I imagine he would have rolled his eyes if he had had any. "I'm more like a bus driver. I got my route. Sometimes I pick up people, sometimes it's empty."

He looked around at his carriage. "Lot of the time it's empty." He touched the back of his skull, as if he forgot he had no hair to smooth. "Like now, for instance."

I noticed his bones were worn smooth and yellowed in some areas, not the bleach white I would expect.

"How much... is the fare?" Kevin said, breathless but his eyes lucid.

"You've paid it." The skeleton turned and walked towards the carriage.

"Let's go," Kevin said, pulling at my arm. "What's that smell?"

To avoid the question, I asked him, "Where does it go?"

"To the waylaid way-stations," he said. "All the lost and unused places of the world. But it comes back; we can always get back."

The skeleton was boosting himself back up to his seat. If he had just leapt back into his seat, I wouldn't have gone. But it was a struggle and, while climbing up the stone wheel, he got his foot caught in a crevice. There was a small snap as he yanked it out and a small white bone, perhaps a toe, fell to the tracks.

"Fuck," the skeleton sighed, and sat down.

My curiosity hit a critical mass with that, and my limbs moved towards the carriage.

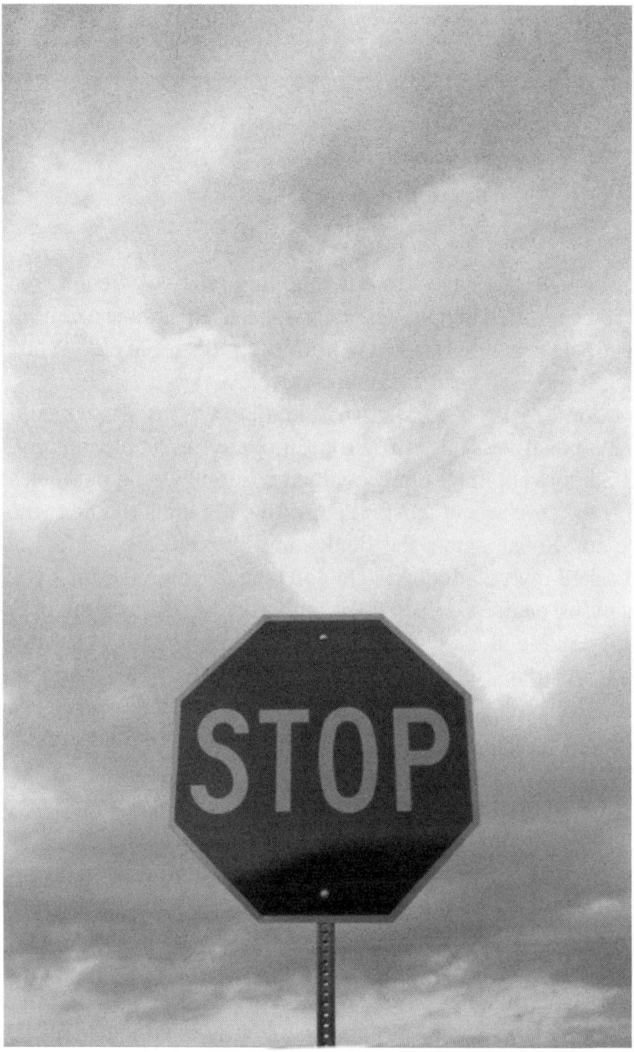
STOP

# Parma Style

Madeleine Baran

Some people have a ton of annoying relatives. People you can't stand to be around. People who treat vegetarianism like a cult religion, or keep asking, "Now, when you say, 'unemployed', you mean looking for a good business opportunity?"

I don't really have relatives like that. On my dad's side, I have ridiculous relatives. Eastern European relatives. People like my great-grandfather, who, in a fit of Slovakian wisdom, would put rock salt on his legs to "cure" rheumatism. People like my grandmother, who went by the non-Polish name, Pat Banks, until her wedding day. When the priest asked my grandfather, "Do you take Appelonia Bankievitz to be your lawful, wedded wife?" my grandfather responded with one word: "Who?" People like a distant relative who was once observed putting out his cigarette on his wife's arm during a backyard wedding reception. People like the mob of relatives who broke out in a serious fistfight over possession of a roll top desk at a relative's funeral several decades ago.

The whole gang congregated in Parma, Ohio, a working class, steel mill town full of ranch houses with aluminum siding, long lines at convenience stores to buy lottery tickets, and one damn good Polish deli.

Every few summers, our family would make the trek from Milwaukee to Parma.

My dad, the oldest son, had left Parma years ago, becoming the first person in the history of the Baran family to go to college. During the summer, he returned, working as a secretary at the steel mill. Setting the precedent for my own bizarre class relations, he spent his breaks reading Rimbaud.

His two brothers stayed. One worked at a water purification plant. The other first ran away to join the circus, then later returned to Parma, spending half his time working at the steel mill and the other half collecting unemployment.

My grandfather's house was our destination. We always called him JB. He was a tall man, with thinning gray hair and a perpetual smirk. To say that he was a character conjures up an image of a jolly old grandfather. JB was a character—but Parma style.

He once went to the doctor complaining of severe stomach pains. When the doctor asked him what he had been eating, he said, "Salami and apples."

The doctor asked, "How many apples?"

"Oh, about a dozen or two," he replied.

"Every week?"

"No. Every day."

He caused a scene at the Ground Round when a waitress made the mistake of putting rice on his plate. He looked around the table at us and said, "What is this stuff?"

"It's rice," my dad replied.

"Oh no. Oh no. I can't eat this stuff, Jimmy. I just can't eat this stuff."

"Well, then, don't eat it."

"Oh no, I don't want this stuff, Jimmy," he said, and called our waitress over to the table.

"What's the problem, sir?" she asked.

"It's this stuff," he said, pointing to the menacing white mass, precariously encroaching on his steak. "I can't eat this stuff."

The waitress seemed confused. My dad's face was bright red. "Would you like me to remove it from your plate?"

"Oh yes," JB responded, relieved to be free from this dangerous, exotic delicacy.

JB once went into the Cleveland Art Museum, paid, went to the gift shop, then the bathroom, and left. The next time he went, with our family, he loudly remarked, in all seriousness, "Oh, so they have paintings in here? The last time I was here, they just had a gift shop."

He also made a statement that caused a security guard to try (and fail) to hold back his laughter. "Now, Jimmy, they've got bee-ooo-tiful stuff in here, but it's nothing compared to Vegas. Have you seen that Taj Mahal they've got there?"

JB was almost entirely deaf. You could hear the television in the back of the house from the front sidewalk. He would lie back in his EZ

Boy recliner, and watch hours of sports on his ridiculously large television set. At the sight of any black man on television, be he Martin Luther King, Nelson Mandela, or Stevie Wonder, JB would say to my dad, "Hey, Jimmy, is that that Ray Charles guy?"

He still lived in the two-bedroom house where my dad grew up. The living room featured thick shag carpeting and a large fake bronze sculpture of an elephant.

Downstairs in the basement, JB had set up a bar, complete with shot glasses featuring naked women, an old jukebox that always got stuck on "That's What Friends Are For" ("And you can… And you can… And you can…"), and a photo of his ex-girlfriend with the words "Wanted $10,000 Reward." (His wife had died before I was born.) One entire wall was covered in a panoramic wallpapered photograph of a lake. Hanging in front of the fifteen-foot long panorama, JB had strategically placed stuffed squirrels, birds, fish.

Every year, within twenty-four hours of arriving in Parma, the discussion would begin. "Hey, Jimmy, let's take a drive out to Amish country," JB would suggest, pronouncing the "a" in Amish like the "a" in amiable. Groans were met all around, but it was no use. "There's this bee-oooh-tiful restaurant out there, Liz," JB would say to my mom. "Best chicken I've ever had."

We'd pile into JB's Lincoln Continental, with the windows rolled up and the air conditioner off. After an hour, tempers were raised.

"I thought you said this place was an hour away."

"It's just a little bit further."

Half an hour later, "Come on, how much longer is this going to take?"

"Just up the road a little bit."

"This is ridiculous."

Sighs all around.

Two hours later, and desperation had sunk in. We were going to be driving around rural Ohio for the rest of our lives, sweating in a Lincoln Continental, stuck to the leather seats. Our bodies would be discovered by an Amish family, and we would be posthumously tortured for intruding on their culture. In the obituaries, the nation would be riled up against us. "Imperialist Family Tries to Exploit Traditional Culture, Dies." Even Barbara Walters would shake her head and call our deadly journey "misguided."

Finally, about three hours into the trip, JB would say, "Here we are. Amish country. First person to spot an Amish buggy gets a nickel!"

When I was younger, my sister and I would climb over each other, peering into the distance, hoping to find any evidence of Amish life, buggy-ed or otherwise. Finally, someone would spot it and JB would point. "There! There! Who saw it first?" as we peered into the eyes of an irate Amish man.

As I grew older, this was easily the most uncomfortable part of the trip. The reward had not risen to meet inflation and the upscale demands of a twelve-year-old. I could no longer bring myself to participate for a mere nickel. (I do not pretend that I would not have climbed over my sister, suffocating her, to spot an Amish buggy for the more reasonable price of, say, five dollars.)

But JB would still yell. "Look! Look! There, behind the corn fields," and all of us couldn't help but turn around quickly to try to get a glimpse. After an hour or so of this, we'd reach the restaurant "with the best chicken in the world." After four hours of driving, we'd eat mediocre, home-style food (with nary a grain of rice to be seen) and then pile back in the car for four or five more hours of sticky-leather-seat-induced misery.

It was the same every year. After a trip to Amish country, a dinner at Chuck E. Cheese (the highlight of the trip), and a visit to the one-story mall, we would leave one Midwestern town for another. It was back to civilization—Milwaukee style.

JB died four years ago. He was above all else, a ridiculous man. Not the best father, but a better grandfather. He saw his wife die, his oldest son die, and his relationships with his other two sons deteriorate.

This wasn't the East Coast. JB didn't start seeing a therapist. Appear on *Oprah*. Take up yoga. Or Feng Shui. It was hard. But he ate a few dozen apples, watched "Ray Charles" on television, and kept his feelings to himself.

He was the last of the bizarre Baran clan. That is, unless I decide to pour rock salt on my legs or adopt a militant anti-rice stance. We'll see.

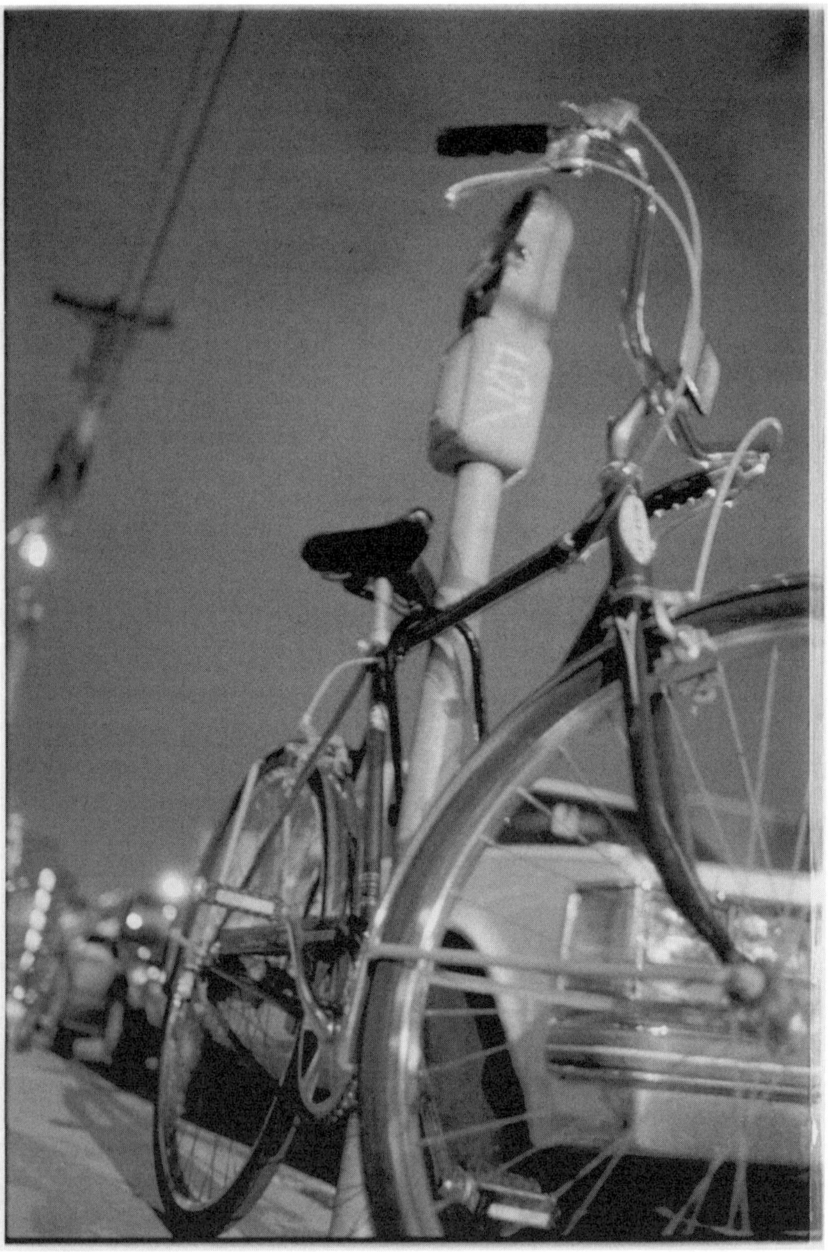

# The New Kid Has an Old Bicycle

Wred Fright

*As Bill counts down each front granite step, he stops and pictures it in his head so he can remember it later. His eyes trace the line of each crack as it winds its way up, around, and down the step, feeling the rise and fall of each bump. Every crack and bump. Bump and crack. Crack and bump. He wants to get it right because each step differs from the others. Individual. He frames the step.*

*Click!*

*Four.*

*They are leaving the house, but he is taking it with him. In his head. He wants to take it apart red brick by red brick, white board by white board, and put it back together when they get to New Castle, but Mom and Dad say it won't fit in the car or moving truck. It won't fit. It won't fit. It just won't fit, they tell him. You can't pack a house in a box like you can a bunch of comic books or matchbox cars. "Besides," they say, "the house will miss its other friends—the trees, the birds, the houses next door, and the street—if we take it with us."*

*Click!*

*Three.*

*The house and he are good friends, too. That's the problem. Bill doesn't want to leave his friend behind. For the first six years of his life, it's all he's ever known. He can't imagine life without it. No matter where he and Mom and Dad went, they always came back to it. The house is a part of him like his arm or his leg or his face. How can he just leave it behind?*

*Click!*

*Two.*

*He can't. Since he can't take the house with him in the car like his comic books and matchbox cars, he decides to take it with him in his head. That's something anyway. That's something at least. At least something anyway. Mom and Dad have snapshots of the house, but it isn't the same. The house looks small in the pictures, penned in, lifeless. By taking the house with him in his head, it remains huge and filled with life. It will still be a part of him. In his head forever. So he swallows the house piece by piece in his head, chewing it with his eyes so that he will he will he will remember it.*

*Click!*

*One.*

*Mom and Dad come down the steps with the last of the boxes and bags. Before they reach him and take him too, he spins around, trying to take it all in. But it's not the same. Everything's different at this early hour. The usually busy street in front of the house is quiet. The sun is just poking its head above the earth, beginning to flood the neighborhood with light, instead of sitting at the top of the sky. There's no Aunt Eleanor on the porch reading her newspaper. And the neighborhood kids aren't playing, running, screaming, laughing. Bill stops spinning and, dizzy, takes a long look at the house. When it stops moving, he waves goodbye.*

*Mom tousles his hair while Dad loads the last box into the trunk of the big red car. The trunk closes with a* thump! *Mom opens up the back door and says, "Get in kiddo, it's time for the big adventure."*

*They are leaving musical Phil-a-del-phi-a for growlly New Castle. Dad gets in and starts the car. Vroom! Vroom! Mom and Dad look at each other and then at Bill.*

*Big red car eases out of the driveway onto the street. Sitting in the back seat, Bill turns and looks at the house through the rear window. Light from the rising sun frames the house, making the face of it dark and sad. Bill turns away from it. He leans forward and stretches his arms across the back of the front seat, and says, "Where we going, buddies?"*

*Mom and Dad laugh, and Mom says, "We're off to our new home, Bill. Aren't you excited?"*

*Bill nods and sits back. He looks out the back window at the house, behind him, already growing smaller. Home. What is home? A place he lives? A place he goes? He never thought it could be a place he leaves.*

*They drive on. The house moves from him. The sun shines brighter but Bill keeps his eyes on the house. He watches it move into the distance and fade until there is nothing but the sun the sun the sun.*

## *Bicycle*

Bill Falcon stood in the woods watching other kids fly into the air on their bicycles. Beams of sunlight reflected off the metal spokes of the rims as they went off the ramp in the middle of the alley and onto the sky. The day was springwarm, and Bill heard the distant roar of the Neshannock Creek as he watched a couple of kids put back together the splintery boards and the rough pile of dirt, stones, and bricks that made up the ramp. It fell apart about every other jump. After it was fixed, a kid backed to the starting line—scraped out earlier by a sneaker dragged across the dirt and gravel of the alley—and pedaled furiously, until the kid hit the ramp and was launched into the air. Back at the starting line, a new row of kids formed to take turns jumping. Bill stepped forward, almost out of the woods, but caught himself, and stepped back to his hiding place among the trees, remembering.

The bicycle had been a gift from his cousins in New York. A hand-me-down. Mom and Dad and he had visited his Aunt and Uncle and cousins in New York last August right before they had moved from Philadelphia. Dad had tied the bicycle to the roof of the big, red car minutes before they had waved goodbye to Uncle, Aunt, and the three descending in size cousins with dark hair and glasses, Cousin 1, Cousin 2, and the one not much bigger than Bill, Cousin 3. Mom had wanted to leave the bicycle behind when they had moved a week later to New Castle. She had said, "It's too big for him! And as usual, it's something they don't want because it's in bad shape."

But Bill had begged and begged and begged and begged and had pleaded and pleaded and pleaded and pleaded, and even had sobbed and sobbed and sobbed and sobbed, and Mom had sighed and Dad had put it in the moving truck.

He had learned to ride it the rest of that summer and that fall, always under the eyes of at least one parent, but then winter had come and Dad, with springtime promises of repair, had put the bicycle away in the shed connected to the back of the new house. He even had promised a new paint job for it to replace the faded red that most closely resembled a mixture of rust and dried blood. "After your father fixes it up and we know it's safe," Mom had said smiling, "you can ride it whenever you want."

But spring had come, and the bicycle remained untouched in the shed. Likewise, Dad remained in his wintertime position, day by day sinking deeper and deeper into his notsoeasychair with the television set blaring away. And each day, as Bill neared the new house after suffering through a day at the new school, he resolved to ask Dad to fix the bicycle, and each day as he approached the back of the notsoeasychair, he changed his mind and instead sat on the couch quiet in the noise of the television, remembering Mom's words, "After your father fixes it up and we know it's safe, you can ride it whenever you want," and remembering words she had said to him later, "It's a tough time for your father right now, Bill, so try not to disturb him. He'll work it out in his own way."

But all the while spring rolled on—March turned to April, and April now threatened to turn to May—the weather becoming warmer in jerks and fits, until finally even the stubbornest of the dirty snow clumps melted, but Dad stayed put, and the bicycle sat and sat and sat and Bill stood and stood and stood and that was that.

Standing still was impossible! Bill shook the images away. He watched one more kid jump into the air, and then Bill turned in the direction of the new house. He walked slowly, kicking the dirt and stones of the path in the woods which ran alongside the alley.

Bill wondered if Indians had walked this path years ago and imagined himself a Monongahela brave on a scouting mission. He tossed a few stones into the ravine and lifted a few logs in search of game and hidden treasure. He tired of this and turned into the Flash. He ran around the world not once but twice! and returned to the exact spot he had started from, and continued his way to the new house at a more leisurely pace. His family was eating late tonight, as Mom had a meeting to attend at St. Peter's, and Dad hardly noticed him anymore, so he was in no rush.

Crossing Graceland, the street between the alley where the kids flew on their bicycles and the alley behind the new house, Bill decided that no matter what, no matter doggone what! when he got to the back of the notsoeasychair he would ask Dad to fix the bike.

The key to the new house lay hidden under some garden tools on a shelf in the shed. When they first moved here, Bill always used to get it after school because no one would be home to let him in. Now, Dad was always home, but Bill continued to get the key from the shed so as not to disturb him. Upon opening the shed door, he saw the bicycle buried under a couple of snow shovels, tangled coils of garden hose, and some dirty lawn clipping bags. He grabbed one side of the handlebars, felt the rubbery grip for a few moments, and then let go. He found the key beneath the garden tools.

When Bill opened the door to the house, he heard the television set blaring. He went into the living room. Dad was still in his pajamas watching a western. Bill sat down on the couch and Dad looked up at him in surprise, as if he didn't recognize Bill.

Bill watched the television with false intensity—the sheriff was talking to a woman—feeling his father looking at him. "Do you want anything to eat?" Dad asked.

"No thanks," Bill said.

They watched the movie. The sheriff gunned down a couple of men in the saloon, and then leapt on a horse outside to chase the one who had slipped out the back. They rode wildly outside of town, guns blazing, dust rising.

During a commercial, Bill went to the kitchen and poured himself a glass of milk. More gunshots came from the living room as he drank it. He washed out the glass and put it upside down in the drainer, and then went back to the living room. He stood by the notsoeasychair, watching the movie some more. The sheriff caught up to the bad guy and shot him down. The sheriff winked to the big bull nearby and rode off into the sunset. Another commercial came on and Bill spoke up, "I'm going to go back out. What time should I be home?"

Dad leaned back, stretching, and looked at the clock on the wall. He furled his brow, then spoke. "Your mother should be back by 7:30. Try to be back by then. She doesn't like it when you're out late."

"Okay," Bill said.

He kissed Dad on the cheek, brushing heavy stubble, almost a beard, and ran out the door.

Once outside, Bill swung around the corner of the house, and moved, careful not to make noise, to the shed. Slowly opening the door, he saw the bike. Breath in sharp bumps, he took it out, untangling it from the garden hose, moving the snow shovels and dirty lawn bags out of the way, and praying to God, Jesus, the Holy Ghost, the Virgin Mary, St. Peter, and everybody else he could think of that Dad wouldn't pick now to rise finally from his wintertime hibernation, or that Mom wouldn't get home from the church meeting early. He leaned the bike in the grass—no kickstand—and put back the hose, shovels, and bags. He set his key back under the garden tools and shut the door.

Bill rolled the rickety bicycle up the driveway and down the hill of his part of the alley, but stopped when he came to Graceland, the road that ran in front of his house. He wanted to get on the bike then, but Mom had warned him about crossing Graceland too many times. Cars sometimes flew by fast around the curve. He thought about turning around and bringing the bike back, but he heard the kids whooping and hollering ahead, just out of sight. He quickly looked both ways—up and down the street—and bolted across Graceland, more dragging than pushing the bike along. When he was safely across the street, he slowed and pulled the bike up to him.

Bill put his left foot on the left pedal and began to swing his right foot over the seat when he looked up and saw the many eyes upon him. He dropped his feet to the ground and leaned forward, pushing the bicycle ahead of him like a shield. The other children laughed as he rolled the rusty, red bike up the alley—the wheels shook, the frame groaned, and the pedals squeaked in rhythmic protest—but Bill knew it could fly.

The kids gathered around the bike when he pushed it up to the line, nearly dividing him from it. He clung to the handlebars with his right hand. The other kids ran their hands along the bike, asking questions, and laughing.

"Where'd you get this?"

Short, dark kid.

"Who are you?"

Girl with glasses.

"What the hell kind of bike is that, man?"

Blonde, spitting in the dirt.

"I've seen you around before—don't you go to Magill?"

"Ain't that too big for you?"

"What's your name?"

"Are you really going to jump on that thing?"

Bill nodded and nodded, not saying a word, until the talk slowed and one voice—deeper and broader than the rest—stood out from the others. "What did you say your name was, kid?"

The oldest boy rolled his bike, a green ten-speed, forward, and the other kids made way for him. He leaned over his bike, resting his elbows on the center, straight part of his curved handlebars, with his long hands drooping motionless, almost touching his front wheel, and his long, dirty, brown hair swaying in the breeze. He looked the red bicycle over slowly. Bill grabbed the red bicycle with both hands again, and said, "Bill. My name is Bill."

The oldest boy looked Bill over, as carefully as he had the bike, before he spoke again. When he did, one of his long hands came alive, and reached towards Bill. "Bill, pleased to meet you. My name's Harris. This your bike?"

Bill nodded and they shook hands. Harris's hand was caked in dirt, and as soon as they had finished shaking, it dropped back to his front wheel. Harris looked the red bike over again, and then said an automatic "Want a cigarette?" as he drew one from his shirt pocket.

Bill shook his head. The cigarette looked flat and crushed. Harris pulled some matches out of his jeans pocket and struck one, the flame faint in the afternoon sun. The cigarette hung limp in his mouth. He lit it, and leaned back on his seat. "Bill, I'll tell you what," he said, blowing smoke in the air. "I was going to take a jump, but now I'm going to sit here and smoke a cigarette. So if you want to take my turn at the ramp, feel free."

The other kids backed away. Bill was alone at the sneaker-scraped line. Harris sat parked behind him, heels in the dirt. Bill saw the ramp in front of him. Awkwardly, he threw his right leg over the seat of the bike. His feet dropped to the pedals, and he felt the seat rise up beneath him. The pedals swung around with a creak. "He's going to kill himself on that thing," Bill heard someone say as he pushed off towards the ramp.

He was moving, moving, moving, like the sheriff on his horse, like the Flash, towards the ramp, towards the sky, a red streak. He pumped the pedals faster and faster. He knew he could fly like the other jumpers. Shoot off the ramp into the sky.

The ramp came closer, getting larger. It wasn't as small as it had looked from the woods. It was immense now, like the entire alley curved up into the sky. He couldn't tell which was which. His front wheel hit the wood with a loud kerthunk! Bill felt the bike rise. He pulled up on the handlebars like he had seen the other riders do.

The sky swallowed him. Wind rushed past. The seat pulled away from him. His legs straightened. He saw the trees and ground rip away. Bill looked up, searching for the sun.

Still looking up, Bill came back to earth with a hard jolt. He pulled back on the pedals to brake, and, hanging onto the handlebars, skidded to a stop. The kids were yelling, but he couldn't tell what they were saying. Bill turned the bike around and pedaled back to them. They grinned at him and offered their hands. He stuck his hand out to shake, but it got slapped.

High fives, like on television. High fives, low fives, all the way around fives.

Bill breathed heavily, resting on his handlebars. Harris rolled up to him, cigarette still hanging limp, but smaller now. "Way to go man," he said, slapping Bill on the back.

Harris rolled forward and squeezed Bill's front tire. He looked at the back tire. "Get those pumped up. That's why you landed so hard," he said, throwing his cigarette to the ground and pedalling away to take a jump.

Everyone took turns jumping then. Each time Bill went he tried to go a little higher and a little farther, always taking a look at the moving sky and world, and then he would pedal back and line up again. As he waited, Bill watched the sun slowly disappear over the squat houses on the hill above the alley, turning redder and hanging lower with each wait. Soon the voices of parents were heard calling kids to dinner. Bill cocked an ear, half-expecting to hear his mother's voice calling him, screaming, upset—"I've been calling you for half an hour! I was worried sick, where have you been!"—but he didn't.

Soon there was hardly any wait to jump at all, and Bill was jumping constantly. Only two other kids were left—Harris and a sandy-haired boy about Bill's age and size named Joe Notascar—and Harris had stopped jumping. Joe stopped jumping as well, and after one last jump, Bill stopped also. They sat on their bikes talking loudly for a few minutes, before Harris looked at the ramp and said, "Might as well take this down. A car might come by."

They tore the ramp apart. Harris lifted the boards and tossed them roughly into the woods while Bill and Joe kicked the stones away and tramped the dirt down. All three tossed the bricks into the woods where they landed in clouds of dust, to be gathered another day. The three boys lingered, looking into the woods. Bill sat on his bike, making sure it was over, reluctant to leave his new friends. Harris spoke then. "You guys got anywhere to be?"

"What else is there to do?" Joe asked.

"I was thinking of trying Suicide Run before it gets dark," Harris said.

Bill, curious, "Where's Suicide Run?"

"It's over in the woods across Graceland." Harris pointed.

Bill followed Harris's finger.

"That's right where I live!" Bill said.

"Uh huh," Harris said. "It's cool. It's not the whole woods, just the little path that runs down the middle from the swamp to the alley. It's rocky and tough with tree roots everywhere, and has a sharp drop off at the end. It'll mess you up if you're not careful. You guys want to give it a try?"

Joe and Bill looked at each other, shrugged, nodded.

"Great! Let's go!" Harris said and rode away.

Bill and Joe followed.

When they came to Graceland, Harris gave it barely a look, and crossed boldly, face forward. Behind him, Joe did the same. Bill looked twice and listened for cars before he crossed. Harris was already on his way up the hill. He stood up on his pedals, turning them slowly as he leaned into the short but steep hill. Bill, too, tried to ride his bike up the hill, but it was hopeless—too steep. He was relieved when he saw Joe leap off his bike in disgust, almost letting it drop to the ground. Joe looked back at Bill and waved for him to catch up. They both ran with their bikes, reaching Harris at the top of the hill, where he was paused, breathing heavily, slouching on the handlebars. He lit another cigarette. Another red glow in the dusk.

Bill pointed out where he lived, excited to show it to his new friends, and Harris, getting off his bike, pointed out where Suicide Run ended. It was just a few feet away from where the driveway to the house began, at one of the main entrances to the woods. They began to walk toward the woods. Bill saw that the big, red car wasn't at the bottom of the driveway so Mom wasn't home yet. He smelled the oil on the gravel, still strong after a couple days. Every time the city coated the alley, Mom said it reminded her of growing up in Mahongingtown, when she and her sisters used to chew soft tar from the roads when they were freshly coated. She said it was thick and dark and soft. Bill imagined it was like the thick, impossible-to-chew gum that came with baseball cards and felt an ache in his jaws as they entered the woods.

It was dark in the woods. Only slender figures of red sunlight danced behind the trees. The tires of the bikes whooshed softly as the boys rolled their bikes in the grass. Harris walked and lightly whistled in the breeze while Joe and Bill kept close behind. The branches of the trees swayed in waves. Soon, they reached the swamp, which smelled of gasoline. Harris stopped and got on his bike. "This is it," he said. "Suicide Run."

"It's not very long," he said with a wave, "it's just tricky with all the rocks and roots. And then there's that little dropoff at the end. Man, if you can jump that, you can fly."

He pushed off then, leaving his words hanging in the air behind him.

They watched him hang on as the roots and rocks jolted his wheels. They saw him pull up on the handlebars and then he disappeared out of the woods through the trees. They listened nervously for the sound of his landing, but heard nothing.

A dog barked.

Harris yelled something.

"What did he say?" Joe asked.

Harris yelled again. This time they understood him. "Next!"

Bill and Joe looked at each other. "I've never ridden this before, man," Joe said. "You want to go first?"

Bill didn't say anything.

Harris yelled again.

"Are you going to do it on that thing?" Joe asked, pointing to the red bicycle.

Bill shrugged. "What else? It's my bike."

"I tell you what," Joe said. "If you're going to do it, I'll do it, too."

Bill nodded.

"Who goes first?" he asked.

"We could flip a coin like they do in football," Joe said.

Bill searched his pockets. "I don't have any money."

"I've got a dime," Joe said. "Call it in the air."

"Heads," Bill said as Joe sent it into the air.

They watched it twirl and drop into the grass. They looked down, but couldn't see it. Bill got down on his hands and searched, his fingers cool in the short, spring grass while Joe bent over and scanned the ground.

"C'mon! What's taking so long?" Harris yelled.

Bill was still running his fingers through the grass when Joe said, "Never mind, I'll go first. Let me know if you find my dime."

Joe got on his bike and pushed off. Bill watched him disappear down the path. He heard a shout and a crash, and then Harris laughing.

"What happened?" Bill shouted.

Nobody answered. Bill breathed heavily.

Then Harris, "Next!"

Bill got on the bicycle, heart in throat. He pedaled and picked up speed. He knew he could do it. He knew he could. The bicycle picked up speed. Bill felt it twist under him as it bumped and rolled over the roots and rocks. He hung on as it moved faster, careening through the woods. A blurred sea of green and black. He tried to put on the brakes, but he slipped forward off the seat, landing on the bar that ran between the seat and the front wheel, and lost hold of the handlebars. He wrapped his arms around that bar, straining for a grip, the bicycle still moving forward through the woods. He bounced on and off the bar, feeling pain, and his feet began to drag on the ground.

Coming out of the woods, Bill shot into the air clinging to the bicycle. He was already crying before he hit the ground, and hit it hard with the bicycle on top of him. His jeans ripped as he skidded, skin and blood smearing from his knees across the alley. He smelled the oil from the gravel close under his face and he clawed roughly at the grass at the edge of the alley where he ended up. Footsteps ran towards him. Joe and Harris were yelling. He ignored them. Embarrassed, burning, he tried to get up. He felt more pain at his center. Someone tried to help him, but he pushed him away. He flailed his feet, kicking the bike off, bawling, blood streaming down his face, knees, thighs. He ran down the driveway towards the house, screaming and crying.

Before he could even knock, the door opened.

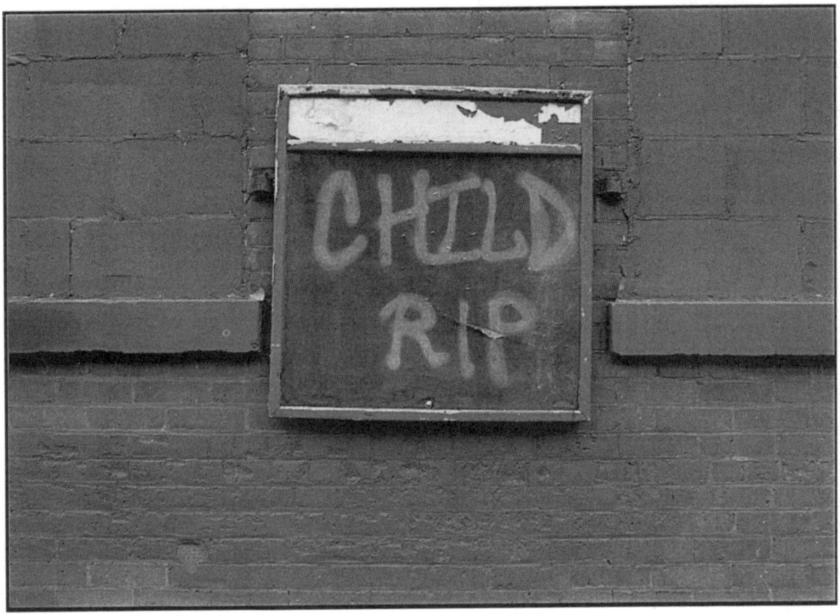
CHILD
RIP

# A Terrible Thing in a Place like This

Jim Ruland

The Floor Boss scampers up the ramp and gives the signal. Pap maneuvers the levers to the iron-spring doors, shunting a terrified heifer into the pens. The Floor Boss presses the snickersnee into my hands. The massive iron sledge is mottled with dried blood and old fear. Its smell is vaguely womanish. I test the snickersnee's weight, measure my grip, swing. The cow's skull collapses, putting me in mind of a sinkhole. The cow settles to the floor, too stunned to know she's dead. The Floor Boss slaps me on the back. *Great Mother of Christ! A son of Cork could not have struck it better!* The florid Irishman hires me on the spot. Pay is a dollar and a half a day.

*

The cows are brought in six at a time. We work in pairs, with knockers at each end of the rickety catwalks. All day long I bludgeon cows. Their heads make a sound like air escaping a bag held underwater. I work fast, faster than my comrades, and by mid-afternoon I'm knocking down four to their two. Blood-bespattered butchers aproned in glistening oilskins cut bellies open. Offal tumbles from slashed cavities. Nothing is wasted. Even the blood pooling at the butchers' ankles is swept into a scupper that empties into the sausage works. *This is a factory,* the Floor Boss shouts at no one in particular, *you're not killing cows; you're making meat!*

*

On my third day at Mackenzie Refrigerator Meats & Sausage, a worker falls into the hog vats and a great roar rises up from the floor. Stink McGrew, a veteran knocker with a long gray beard, sets his snickersnee down on the scaffold. *Come on, boyo,* he says to me, *let's go have ourselves a look.* Stink elucidates the finer points of hog slaughter as we make our way across the pens. *They cut 'em open, trammel the carcass and hoist 'em into a vat of boilin' brine. The soup loosens the bristles, see? Makes it easier to scrub 'em off before they're quartered and sent to market. Hogs are hard to kill, boyo. They shit and piss and discharge great quantities of filth when they hit the soup. Mind yourself. That's the last place you'd want to be fallin'.* A throng of curious workers assembles at the edge of the vats. The Floor Boss uncorks a bottle of Chadwick's Unadulterated and passes it to Pap. The worker surfaces, his face swollen, fit to burst. He whips an arm up over the lip of the cauldron as if to hoist himself out, but there's no feeling left in his limbs, his fingers claim no purchase, and he's sucked back down into the roiling muck. I move to assist but Stink stops me, shaking his head gravely. The Hog Master barks orders at the Italian work party that rushes to get him out. The Floor Boss sermonizes: *Almighty Father, we beg you to bless this low scoundrel, this clumsy, sow-slaughtering scum who has sacrificed himself so gracelessly for Mackenzie Refrigerator Meats & Sausage. Forgive him his pride, this scurrilous social climber, for his pitiful offering of Neapolitan stew. Reared in ignorance, poverty and filth, they know not what they do. Amen.* The Floor Boss bows his head, crosses himself and barks: *Workers, workers, man your nets and net your man!* The Italians haul him out of the vat like a great fish. His flesh is horribly discolored, the extremities all but cooked.

*

With two-hundred-fifty feet of frontage on 42nd Street and another two hundred on Packers Avenue, she stands as stolid as a fortress. The Floor Boss, who helped build the place, swears the factory's blue bricks were shipped from Egypt, cooled in the waters of the Nile in the manner of the Pyramids. To the north, tracks connect by private switch to the Grand Trunk Railway where armed cow pinchers sit astride dusty mustangs, restlessly guarding the freight from anarchic factions within the factory. Darius Birch, the prohibitionist, claims the windows in Mr. Mackenzie's house are barred as a precaution against dynamarchists. Stink tells me there's a Gatling machine gun in the Desplaines Street precinct that was paid for with cattle money. Seany Corker swears Mr. Mackenzie opens the payroll offices on the first Sunday of every month to pay off the Pinkertons, but everybody knows Seany hasn't spent a Sunday sober since the Floor Boss caught him in the sheep corral in his balbriggan underwear, banging away on a forty-pound ewe. At the end of the day, the swiftly darkening sky over Chicago transforms the sparkling abattoir into something more beautiful than it has a right to be.

*

I live in a rented room in a lodging house in the south division. Rent is three dollars a week. The proprietor's name is Mrs. Fortunata. Her daughter, Anna, cooks the food. As near as I can tell, there is no Mr. Fortunata in evidence. My room contains a bed, a chipped washbasin, and the books I printed with my own hands when I worked as an apprentice in the Bishop's print shop in the Archdiocese of Baltimore. At night I turn the pages and scrutinize the type with a printer's eye, though it would be a mistake to call it reading.

*

The Floor Boss pulls me off the afternoon shift. He leads me across a secret network of platform planking to a dark and muddy lane behind the sausage works. Three cows stand dumbly in makeshift pens gone shabby with neglect. New England cattlemen size me up like a prime example of horn cattle. The Floor Boss unwraps a new snickersnee with an iron sledge as bright as a diamond. *Three cows. Three blows. Can ye manage it?* I pull on oilskin gloves and go to work. The skull cracks and the blow sends a scalding jet of brain bile into my eyes. The cattlemen laugh at my clumsiness. Their bloodless derision inoculates me with a wild and reckless fury. I move down the pens a blind berserker, all practiced precision, all reason, gone. The last heifer smells me coming, goes spastic with fear. I bring the snickersnee across the top of the crude stable sidewise like a reaper, crushing the heifer's head against the bricks. She hits the floor without so much as a twitch. One of the cattlemen doubles over, empties his stomach on the red flagstones. The Floor Boss cackles until the color rises in his pale, drawn face. Money spills forth in a silvery flash. The Floor Boss gives me five dollars and the rest of the afternoon off. Although it is several hours before my eyesight is properly restored, I spend the afternoon on a grassy slope on Michigan Avenue watching boats glide over the greasy lake.

*

The Floor Boss brings me to the decrepit stables behind the sausage works once a week, sometimes more. Sportsmen, politicians, great ladies of the municipality come to wager against my prowess with the snickersnee. I work shirtless one week, and am outfitted like a gladiator in heavy leathers the next. Afterwards they take me to beer gardens and saloons where I am declared a champion knocker, a good German. *Not like those filthy insurrectionists!* Word of my exploits filters through Mackenzie's. I am befriended by hog slaughterers and beef butchers alike. Friday evenings, Stink and Pap take me to bare-knuckle bouts in the Irish quarter and it takes me the better part of Saturday to feel like myself again, such is their generosity with the Chadwick's. On Sundays I attend church services and temperance meetings with Darius, who warns me against Catholics and the Irish curse. Late one night Pap rousts me out of bed. The Floor Boss waits for me in the street and they take me to a brothel in the Levee. They pay my way and I choose the girl who most resembles Anna. She is a spindly creature easily half my age. In the bedchamber she is willing yet demure; there is no pretense of rapture. Through the thin walls I can hear the Floor Boss striking his boy and I close my ears to their cries.

*

On Saturdays the workers get drunk. Fights break out on the killing floor. Butchers cavort with the carcasses, spinning their trammeled flanks like gay dancers. Cardsharps use a butchered hog as a gaming table. A pair of Austrians roll a wine keg liberated from a freight car into the sausage works. Outside, the rattle of rifle fire can be heard as the cow pinchers try to shoot the ears off a lone bull penned in the stockyards. Throughout the madness the cows come in waves. Their skulls crack open at my feet. Swimming with drink, Stink teeters under the weight of his snickersnee and collapses on the catwalk. I attend to Stink, try to get the old man to sit up, and I observe The Floor Boss crawling out from under an Indian blanket. He opens his drawers and pisses through the planking. Down below the men scatter. *Get back to work, you fecking anarchists!* I take hold of the filthy Indian blanket to keep the flies off Stink and find a naked Italian boy sucking on his thumb. The Floor Boss staggers about with his desiccated manhood exposed, roaring drunk. At shift's end I find the boy some clothes and bring him to Mrs. Fortunata's.

*

After church services Darius takes me to a political meeting at the Lagerbier Hall on West Lake Street. A black flag hangs from the podium at the front of the hall. Watchers eye the exit for police and Pinkertons. A bearded, bespectacled man in a black slouch hat addresses a modest but rowdy crowd. *We will not be overpowered nor overawed. They think their stupidity sacred because it is part of their established order. Not so! Force engenders force! Better to die gloriously in the full heat of battle than to be starved to death on fifty cents a day!* The workers' passions are ignited, but they are more interested in the beer barrel at the back of the hall. When the hat is passed, a drunken Bohemian Sharpshooter crosses his arms and spits on the floor. Disgusted, Darius gives me the signal to leave. A slender young man of neat appearance whom I'd known back in Baltimore greets us at the exit. Overjoyed, I tell him about my work at Mackenzie's. He congratulates me and urges me to attend a meeting at

Turner Hall the following Sunday. Darius creeps toward the door as I take my leave. He twitters with childlike astonishment. *Do you know who that was? Only the most dangerous anarchist in Chicago!*

*

When Pap gives the signal, the knockers climb down from the catwalk. I don't want to leave. The train outside is filled with animals that haven't figured out what is happening to them. There's a question about the billing and the railway inspector won't release the cattle. The cow pinchers double in force. The Floor Boss sends everyone home. I shuffle back to Mrs. Fortunata's. In the alley, a wild dog with a feral, wolf-like countenance noses through the trash. My heart quickens, hot for blood. I unsheathe my knife and creep up on the animal. When it's over, there's a gash under my chin and for reasons that aren't clear to me, the animal's entrails are arranged in a steaming blue pile. I slip my hand inside and still its mongrel heart. Broad beams of light shower the alley. I am an angel striding fearlessly through a dream.

*

The Floor Boss sends word I am no longer needed at Mackenzie's. The messenger reassures me it's only a temporary stoppage. The cold creeps up the shaft of the stairwell. I slip back into sleep and dream I am sitting down to dinner with my mother and father in the parlor of a celebrated writer. My father presents him with a new book from his printing house; the leather covers are red like the blood the words will inspire. The meeting is consecrated with cognac. My mother sends me out of the parlor. I chase pigeons in the plaza, their fluttering shadows as majestic as the Dome.

*

In the street, I am fearful of being jostled, fearful of any contact at all. I marvel at the sight of so many windows thrown open to the cold, the empty frames like the eye sockets of bewitched skulls. A man with flashing eyes approaches. It is my friend from Baltimore. *Come*, he says, *there's something you should see*. He takes me to the offices of the *Arbeiter-Zeitung*—the most radical newspaper in the city. The familiar sights and smells of the printing house leave me shaky. My friend cannot know my father was taken from my home at midnight and hung from a lamppost for printing leaflets critical of Bismarck's anti-socialist law of '78. I stagger forward. He guides me to a cot, begs me to lie in it. I succumb to his kindness. After hours of erratic sleep populated with awful dreams (the Floor Boss in a Kaiser helmet, Anna and the boy strung up in the sausage works), I don't wake so much as rise to the surface of this new reality. A bespectacled fellow reads from a galley sheet; his words thunder in my ears: *We have come to a desperate pass. Political liberty without economic freedom is an empty phrase. Religion, government and capital are carved from the same piece of wood. The time for parliamentary chatter has passed; the time for revolutionary action has begun! Let us pursue the propertied class to their last lurking place and destroy them! We are the lightning! We are the frenzy! Extirpate the wretches! Extirpate them all!*

*

Work at the factory resumes. The Floor Boss asks me about the long stripe of blood below my chin. He takes my evasion to mean I've been sporting with feisty whores. I contemplate the effects of my snickersnee on an Irish skull. Although I've left explicit instructions with Mrs. Fortunata that the boy is not to leave her sight, he returns to Mackenzie's daily. The boy shadows the Floor Boss. Between shifts I stumble over them coupling in the meat locker. During lunch, Stink frets over my injury. He shakes his head in disapproval. *'Tis a terrible thing in a place like this, boyo.*

*

I put in as much time on the presses at the *Arbeiter-Zeitung* as my stamina allows, but the long hours in the pens wear me down. I make arrangements for the boy to spend his days with the newspaper sellers where he'll be safe from the Floor Boss's influence. There are days when the hideous keening from the hog vats follows me to the printing house and refuses to go away. Sometimes it's the flies that threaten to overwhelm me, the never-ending drone of a million iridescent wings. The days grow longer and the cloying odor from the filthy lanes weakens my resolve. I tie a wet cloth to my face lest I lose command of my balance and topple into the pens. At shift's end my arms are like dead tubes that can barely manage the sledge. We wash up with crude, foul-smelling soap manufactured with sow fat and I carry the scent of the pens to my room each night until everything I own reeks of Mackenzie's. On bad days the odor is overwhelming and I end up down in the clerk's office, weeping uncontrollably in Darius's arms.

*

The mechanical doors swing open, the new meat saunters in. One cow stands out from the rest. *Would you look at that one? 'Tis positively massive*, I wait for Stink to comment, but he doesn't say a word. The beast is monstrous. Its thick hide much shaggier than the others'. The creature waddles bear-like into the pens and scratches at the door with great shaggy claws. I peer over the planking for a closer look. The cow's head appears normal enough but the body is all wrong. *What's the matter?* Stink shouts. I want to know if he's ever seen a steer's head on a bear's body before, but I keep my silence. Stink starts a-knocking. His snickersnee drops down on the cows like a pendulum. The cows panic in their pens. Their terror washes over me and breaks with wavelike force. Stink leans breathless on his sledge. *Well, are ye going to work or aren't ye?* It takes a dozen blows to put the bear-cow down. Stink offers the Chadwick's he can no longer do without. *Are ye okay? Do ye need a respite?* I refuse the bottle and reassure Stink, but I worry this event will open the door to new concerns.

*

Without provocation, the police break up a meeting of the Lumber Shovers' Union. A scuffle breaks out. The police fire into the assembly, killing one man, injuring dozens more. A worker draped in blood pushes past me. I'm tripped up by a man being beaten by a pair of policemen and the blows from their puny truncheons rain down on my shoulders. My friend pulls me to my feet, whisks me down the back stairs. Together we sprint through the streets to his dwelling place. His basement apartment has been converted into a workshop. I see coils of fuse, sheet-iron molds, cans of English dynamite. He extracts a composition bomb from the secret bottom of a well-traveled steamer trunk and places it in my hands. Its considerable weight and cool curves feel like history made whole. We race back to the union hall where a dwindling retinue of policemen disperses the stragglers. We're too late. My friend rages, silver eyes agleam. I make no effort to restrain him, but am glad when he takes the bomb from me. *Words are wasted on these men, they respect only deeds*. He holds the bomb up to my face. *Would you sign your name to such a document?* The moon is but a puddle, feeble and dim, next to the metallic fervor blazing in his eyes. *Yes*, I answer, *yes*.

*

At night the slaughterhouse complicates my dreams. All manner of strange beasts shuffle through the pens: bears, lions, rhinoceroses, wolves. Sometimes I pounce from the platform with a curved dagger and hew the flesh with great ferocity. Some nights I move among the stupid beasts in shaggy costume and hack them to bits with an axe. When all my strength forsakes me, I pull on a trap door in the floor and a figure in black rags hands me a bomb with a sputtering fuse. I hurl the machine into the pens and disappear underground. Sometimes I wake breathless and wheezing, the windows in my tiny room thick with moisture, like the insides of a giant lung. Sometimes Anna is there with a damp cloth. If I can't stop screaming, she wedges one of the books between my teeth while her mother's silvery shape, silhouetted by the early sun rising beyond the curtainless window, watches us from the doorway.

*

In his boundless greed, the Floor Boss installs bleachers behind the sausage works so that as many as a hundred sportsmen may attend. Now when I am summoned with my snickersnee, there are six cows instead of three, only they don't look much like cows anymore. All manner of bovine monstrosities prowl these pens. There are cows with the heads of parakeets, baboons, wild boars. Cows that slither on enormous slug-like extremities. Cows with armadillo shells, leopard spots and scales. Cows with grotesque insect heads that stare at me, hatred flashing in their multiple eyes. Cows that gambol on slender hooves. Cows that beat their wings, scattering sheets of flies in the terminal air. Like Adam, I give them names: uni-cow, yakkopotamus, moo-snake. Then there are those rapacious beasts that resemble no species of bovine I've ever encountered: striped stags with panda heads and fearsome tails, or horrible insect-like mammals that disgorge fleshy eggs all over the pens. I engage in wholesale slaughter with everything that moves.

*

Late at night when the boy thinks I'm fast asleep, he brings Anna into my room and takes her in a patch of moonlight. The girl's rapture terrifies me. While the boy's corruption of Mrs. Fortunata's daughter is wrong, wanting Anna for myself is certainly worse. Enthralled by the sight of her black hair spread out in wavy relief against the moon-bleached floorboards, I watch, and in my own private way participate in their passion. This is my terrible secret.

*

Spring brings agitation to the meat factory floor. Mr. Mackenzie cuts wages. The threat of a walk-out gives Mackenzie's masters pause. Darius fears another labor stoppage will necessitate the hiring of scabs, ensuring more violence, more bloodshed. I go with Stink and the others to a rally outside McCormick's Reaper Works. All of the unemployed working men of Chicago are there. Near the speaker's platform, men in sharply angled suits loiter about, conspicuous in the crush of the jobless. A pair of tramps wait for a man smoking a machine-rolled cigarette to drop the butt. The rally goes poorly. The skies darken and many leave early. As the last speaker addresses the crowd, the police move in with the order to disperse, clubbing a path through the mob. A police captain lashes his whip at anyone who

comes near his buggy. A heavy stone glances off my shoulder, clatters at my feet. Enraged, I pick it up and heave the dead mass into the throng. The noise in the street is like nothing I've ever heard. The workers mount an attack with railroad spikes and stones, but a volley of gunfire quells their charge. A policeman standing close enough to knock his hat off shoots Stink in the chest. A scarlet corsage blossoms in the old man's breast and he goes down quick as a heifer. An axe handle finds its way into my hands and I strike the beefy, walrus-faced murderer across the bridge of his nose. A bell sounds as if a hundred mechanical doors have flown open at once. Instinct drives me to the foot of a three-legged zebra; a single swipe puts it down. A dark shadow engulfs me as a giant goat-bat takes wing. I knock it out of the air and destroy it. Tiger-rats, panda-dogs, and fanged baboons converge on me. I stun them senseless with my crude sledge. I dispatch a hyena-worm walking upright on human legs, but a gorilla-finch with fearsome claws takes its place. There are too many of them. Reinforcements from the Desplaines Street precinct arrive on foot and by car. I retreat to an alley. Darius is there. He scratches a match along the brick wall and marries the thin blue flame to the tip of a fuse. He puts the hissing contraption in my hand and disappears. The gibbering horde advances. I curl my fingers around the cool metal and hurl it at the hideous menagerie. There is a moment of absolute stasis as I am suffused with a sense of calm that is available to me only after the boy has finished and Anna crawls across the floor—the wildest creature yet—to find me in the dark. Then,
oblivion.

*

Chicago tumbles off its track, plows backward in time, the township reinventing itself in the image of my hometown where socialists and section men, anarchists and incendiaries decorated the lampposts. The capitalist press howls for blood. The police force obliges. Homes are sacked. Unions disbanded. Presses destroyed. But on Lake Michigan the dreamlike movement of triangular sails across the steel horizon tells me Chicago has not yet gone completely mad. I sleep in boats, railway cars, an abandoned apple cart. I pick up bits of offhand conversation and rearrange them in bold printable type. I pass Mrs. Fortunata on her way to market and she doesn't recognize me. Without Mackenzie's I am a blank face in the herd. I race to her home and crash into the kitchen, ravenous with hunger. The boy is there. Anna, too. There is a bowl of soup on the table. I am angry, but all my senses take me to the gorgeous scent of the soup. I tilt the bowl and drain it. Sated,

I look for the boy, but he is gone and Anna stands weeping by the window.

*

The little boy picks a curious path through the slums. A mild, irrepressible bubble of shame rises in my throat and stays there as he cuts through the empty Haymarket, but the street has no memory. The boy darts inside a saloon I used to frequent with Stink, but Stink is gone. Why do I have such trouble with that? I watch through the window as the boy navigates his way through the tables like he's been there before. He stops at a place where a number of Pinkerton agents are seated and whispers in Darius's ear.

*

My knife sketches a line across the boy's throat. It's not a deep cut, but the blood spurts like ink. The boy doesn't cry out, although I want him to. I stand a massive iron bed frame on end and string him up with a length of rotted rope I found at the wharf. He whimpers and pleads. Gutted, I arrange his organs in neat piles, douse them in lamp oil and set them aflame to keep the rats at bay. He whimpers, begs forgiveness, tells me Darius was in bed with the Floor Boss from the beginning. Yes. This is precisely what I want to hear; his last words are a comfort to me.

*

I am going to the gallows. I know it. My jailers know it. The people of Chicago, such as they are, know it. They think me mad and their low estimation is helped along by my behavior. I can scarcely speak. The festering wound at my throat has ruined my shirt so I scurry about unclothed. I beat my head bloody on the bars and howl at the guards in a language that needs no interpreting. Strange thoughts lurk here. They steal upon me during the lonely hours when even the rats won't have anything to do with me. The events of the past few months, the whole of my experience in Chicago, take on the substance of a dream. I remember elusive fragments only—the brothels, the stockyards, the pens—and the details bring me no anxiety. The only constant is the ceaseless hunger gnawing at my guts. On the eve of my execution I receive an unexpected visit from my old, old friend. He stands in the doorway with a bag of oranges, eyes shining. He salutes my courage, my iron will, going on and on how the newspapers of the propertied classes are beginning to editorialize that the horrific working conditions at Mackenzie's surely played a part in my madness. He peels the skin and funnels the fleshy fruit into my mouth. One of the oranges is not right. Its skin comes loose, falls away like the strap on Anna's nightdress, revealing the iron casing of a miniature composition bomb. Louis handles it with practiced delicacy. *Have you ever pondered thus? Would you cheat your fate thus?* He guides it into my mouth. The cool metal presses against my molars. All anger leaves me. My friend and comrade stands poised, match at the ready. He needs a signal. I take a deep breath, lower my head, clack my hooves for the Revolution.

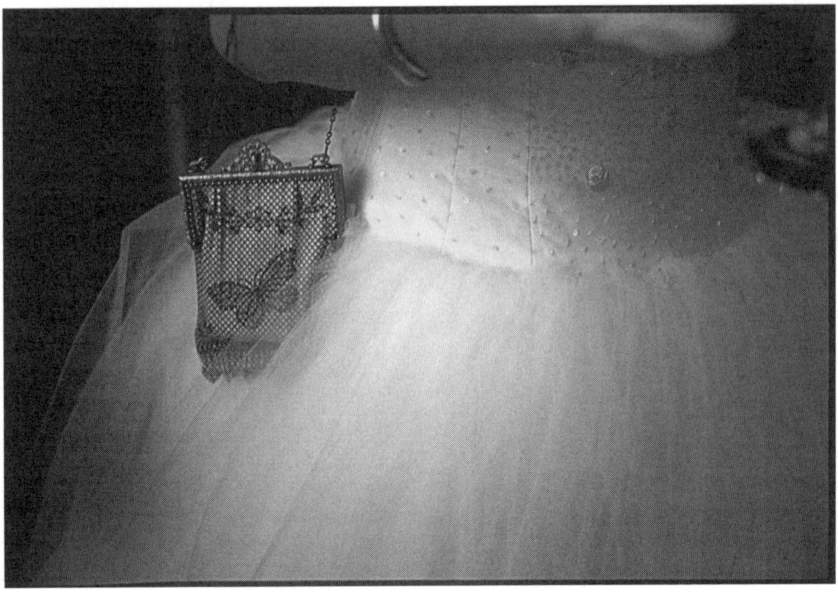

# Our Quincey Cells

Patricia Geary

"Quincey says nobody needs to do it more than once a month," my sister informed us. We were all riding in her more or less new Buick, which was somehow, but not directly, made possible by this selfsame Quincey, and we were on our way to one of those downtown renewal tourist trap places. We knew the approximate location yet all the streets—they never show this on maps—were one way, the other way.

"Then you better watch out," said our mother, Wanda. "I don't even know a single man of my generation who feels that way."

"Suits me fine," said Kim. "Who's got the time?"

I decided not to chime in, especially since I was feeling a little carsick. The huge, bright sky of South Florida was simply too much for all these windows.

"The latest thing is he used to be a preacher. He went to an evangelist summer camp? They spent two and a half full days explaining how to take up the collection."

"I can well believe that," said Rita, my other sister. This information seemed to cheer her up. She had been sitting somewhat morosely on the other side of the backseat, with Kim's daughter between us.

"Here we go," said Kim, swerving into a dinky lot, all cracked asphalt and lime green weeds.

"Seven dollars," said Wanda, ominously.

"I'll pay." I rooted in my purse and stuffed the bills forward before they could get cranking about the details.

"Every time I see her, Clare's got to subsidize me," Kim protested.

"You drove all the way down. I don't mind."

"I've got a dollar here somewhere," said Rita, fumbling in her bag. She carried an oversized decorated satchel. None of them could ever find their wallets.

"Let me pay," I said. "But couldn't we park in the covered area?"

"I like this one," said Wanda, and that was that.

The sky was pre-rain, and you could smell those roiling clouds in from the Gulf. When I got out of the car, drops splattered on my sunglasses.

"What's wrong, you going to melt?" Rita asked. She was wearing a large floppy hat that she'd decorated herself with feathers, chains, and patches.

"I hate this," I said, running ahead of the pack. "Meet you over there." I took off and only Abbie, my niece, kept pace. We didn't know each other very well and she was watching me.

The shelter we ran to opened onto a street, which was already teeming with tourist traffic. An electric violin whined forth from a nearby shop, but it was nearly drowned out by the honky-tonk piano from Rosie O'Grady's "saloon."

"Here's where I got my moccasins," said Rita, guiding us into a western-themed store: spittoons, bear heads, stuffed rattlesnakes, and so on.

"Just what you wanted, huh?" Kim said. "Like you don't have this stuff out where you live. Don't touch that, Abbie."

"What is it?"

"It's made out of bull testicles."

I gazed around the large space chockablock with stuff. Some of my queasiness came back.

"I could spend a week in here," said Kim, wandering off. Rita had already disappeared into the overpriced Indian jewelry.

"Listen," I said to Wanda. "I'll be outside."

"This isn't for me, either."

Outside, the rain was really kicking in. "These stores are like casinos," I said. "No windows, all that noise."

"I love Las Vegas," said Wanda.

We all met up again inside the so-called mall, which was adjacent to the renovated downtown. There were a few real stores, chain names that I recognized, but most of the spaces sold ceramic clowns and "collectible" dolls dressed like Southern belles and cut-off tee shirts with sequined palm trees. I was sitting on a bench, smoking a cigarette, which I never did at home, and smelling the fresh fudge from the "old-fashioned" candy place.

"I'd like to buy some new underwear," Kim said, joining us on the bench. The simplicity of her unadorned jeans and navy sweatshirt distinguished her from the tourist crowd, and from us. "But that's always the kiss of death for me and a relationship. What I've got I've had for years."

"We just wear plain old cotton now," said Rita.

Wanda nodded solemnly, bracelets jangling and necklaces clinking. "Serviceable. No need for the fancy stuff."

Their joke was that the only man who'd crossed the threshold of their house in the last year or so had been the refrigerator repairman.

"I'm not saying what kind I wear," said Kim.

"Afraid to shock us?" Wanda asked, perking up.

"Not in this crowd."

"Mama, I got to get this dress," said Abbie, running up. Even Abbie, in her pink tee shirt and checked shorts, looked festive next to Kim.

Everyone gazed at her approvingly. Only eleven, but she was on the right track.

"Quincey loves to talk on the telephone," said Kim, lighting a cigarette. She was dyeing her hair blond again, and it looked good. Now she needed to work on her body. "He calls, oh, at least once a day. He can just talk and talk for two or three hours, whether Stephanie's there or not. He can talk about anything. If I'm not there, he'll just talk to Abbie."

"Yeah," said Abbie. "And he does all the talking."

"That's not true," said Kim. "He really listens."

"Sure," Abbie said. "What about that dinner he owes me?"

"He does need to take us out," said Kim, suddenly emphatic. "I mean, I really haven't seen one red cent out of all this. Except when I bought steaks that time, he did pay me back."

"He owes me dinner out," Abbie said. "And, Mama, I want that dress."

"You keep him to that dinner," Kim said. "You make sure and remind him now."

"Who's Stephanie?" I asked. We'd moved our location to a bench outside Abbie's dress shop. On the upper tier of the mall, traffic was sparse, and you could see the sky, still swollen with rain, through the massive windows. After the first burst of energy, shopping with these guys tended to deteriorate into shifting from smoking spot to smoking spot, with a bit of browsing thrown in for diversion.

"He lives with her," said Kim, on my left. "But they don't have sex."

On my right, Wanda and Rita exchanged looks.

"She's this skinny thing from England and she has that bad pasty skin. She won't comb her hair or shave her legs. She doesn't even brush her teeth unless he reminds her."

"Nobody in Europe shaves their legs," I offered, the cosmopolitan traveler. "Shaving's a ridiculous American habit."

"I know some men," said Kim ominously, "who ought to shave their entire bodies."

We all lit up another round, sharing lighters. We were waiting for Abbie, but we weren't in a big hurry to leave. Once we went back to Wanda and Rita's house, Kim and Abbie would have to drive back north. All we ever did was talk anyway, and here was our chance to talk against a fresh backdrop.

"Stephanie's not all there," Kim continued. "Quincey found her by the side of the road when he moved from Jacksonville. He got her off the booze and had her jaw fixed. He says she's really weird, though. Sometimes Stephanie will just walk in a store and go like this." Kim stood up and raised her arms.

"Mama, please," said Abbie, stepping up, shopping bag in hand.

Kim pranced along on the balls of her toes, looking vague and singing la-la-la tonelessly.

"Not all there," Wanda agreed.

"Maybe he won't leave her until she has a baby," I suggested. I knew a little more than I was letting on, having been primed by Wanda and Rita.

"Oh no," Kim said. "Judge made him get a vasectomy."

"With eleven kids—" I began.

"But they're all with different women! And that's not counting the one he found under an overpass."

"That guy," said Rita, "has a real knack for finding things."

"He raised this child for years, just like one of his own. Then he found out who the mother was. Turned out Quincey'd gone to high school with her."

"Thanks, Aunt Clare." Abbie pulled out her dress. She'd chosen well; the cornflower blue would set off her eyes.

"He got the mother off drugs. Bought her a house and her own dry cleaner business. But she just sold the whole thing and went back to drugs. So Quincey figured he'd done all he could. He's a complete teetotaler himself."

Rita snorted loudly. Wanda was busy fingering Abbie's dress, probably checking the seams.

"He never even smoked pot," Kim continued, ignoring Rita.

"What about caffeine?" I asked, just to keep it going.

"Oh, sure. He used to go to bars and drink coffee and watch the guys with the good-looking girls. He'd wait for the guys to get too drunk to drive, then he'd offer to take the girls home."

"He seems to have specialized young," Wanda opined, handing the dress back to Abbie.

"I guess," said Kim. "But he says he's had more than his share of all that. That's why he's with me."

"Quincey's buying me a house," Kim announced on our return trip. The Buick was hot and damp, and I hadn't eaten anything since breakfast. "I found this great house? I called him right up when I found it, and he said who else did you call, and I said nobody, I called you first. And he said good, that's the way it's supposed to be. But he hasn't gone to see it yet."

"Maybe he's getting cold feet." I was tired, and a little mean.

"Oh no," said Kim, unfazed. "This is a business investment for him. He's got money buried all over his backyard. When Stephanie had her mastectomy, he paid cash then and there. Forty thousand."

"Then why does he live in a trailer?" Wanda asked.

"Well," I said, after Kim and Abbie took off. "She seems to be in pretty good spirits, all things considered."

Wanda and Rita were settled in for the evening, Wanda on her couch and Rita in her chair. Their house was cozy and predictably chock-full of "interesting" items: fake chinoiserie, huge bouquets of silk sunflowers, leopard print pillows. If you looked at the stuff item by item, it was tacky—but if you softened your gaze and squinted a bit, you could sink into comfort.

"Yes, she does," Wanda agreed. "This Quincey has done a lot for her ego. Though she says he's a total cracker."

"Big surprise there." I nibbled on some mixed nuts, but they weren't quite doing the trick.

"Where does she find them?" Wanda shook her head and took another sip of her bourbon and coke. She had exactly two every evening, always out of a highball glass. "Put her in a room with two hundred people. She'll find the total cracker."

"A cracker detector," I said.

"And her accent," said Rita, sipping her plain coke. "I lived in New York ten years. I don't speak like the Bronx. I mean I hope I don't."

"You don't," I said. "But Kim always wanted a Southern accent. She picked it up the very first year we moved here."

"You ought to hear her sometimes," Wanda said fondly.

"She gets on a roll," said Rita. "She'll say he don't. She'll say ain't."

"Today was nothing," said Wanda. She snapped her fingers at Rita. "I've got to pee. Tell Clare about what we discovered. Why Kim's changed her whole attitude."

"I'll wait till you get back."

"Okay."

Rita leaned forward after Wanda left. "I'm so happy to see you," she said. "We've missed you so much. It's been too long."

My chest tightened and my eyes burned and then it all passed and I smiled. There were a lot of things I might have said, but I didn't.

Wanda came back in talking. "One day last summer, on one of her visits, we just sat her down."

"And plied her with beers," Rita added.

"We did not ply her with beers," Wanda corrected.

"Anyway, we sat her down, and we said, look, we love you. Do you love us? Well," Rita paused dramatically, and took a large gulp. "She said, I hate myself. I don't think I can love anybody because I hate myself so much. I don't think I ever have loved anybody."

"What did you do?" I'd gone through most of the cashews, picking them out.

"Oh, we just kept telling her we loved her anyway. And then she called just last month, crying and crying, and she said what does Quincey see in me anyway? He says he finds me attractive. But I'm so fat! And I said, yes, you're way too fat. You have a horrible temper, and you're lousy with money. But you have many, many good qualities."

"How did that go over?" I asked dubiously.

"Just great! Now she knows she can trust us. She didn't start screaming or anything."

"I'm craving some chocolate," Wanda announced later.

"When you crave something, then that's what you're allergic to." The longer my visit, the more pompous I got.

"That blows my food theory," Wanda said cheerfully.

We'd been talking about a friend of mine who either was or wasn't an alcoholic. As soon as she had even one sip of wine, she instantly smelled like a distillery.

Rita had been pretty cool about the whole thing. "That's what they say in AA," she'd said a couple times and then dropped it.

"My food theory," Wanda offered, "is eat what you crave. For instance, the cell knows what to do to survive. It knows what it needs."

"But maybe the fat cells aren't so bright," I said. "Like that ghost in Toys'R'Us. I bet the fat cells aren't the smart ones in your body. They're the trailer park dwellers of the cell world. You think they should get to boss the brain cells around?"

"They're my Quincey cells," said Wanda with a note of finality.

"Exactly."

"But I'd still like a little something else to eat."

"You had two drinks, three pieces of pepperoni pizza, and a bowl of peach ice cream." When the words came out of my mouth, I realized how closely I'd been keeping track.

"Better have a little something if you're hungry," Rita said automatically, as if she'd long since tuned us out.

"Why?" I demanded. "It's after ten. Why do you need to eat?" There was so much mutual nourishing going; I felt overstuffed, almost bulimic.

"My Quinceys need feeding," said Wanda. She walked over to the refrigerator and stood there a moment. Although the outside was covered by a massage of cutesy magnets, the inside was perfectly divided; they had separate shelves, separate milk, butter, everything.

She closed the door then, and turned back toward us. "Well," she said, making the best of the situation. "Maybe not."

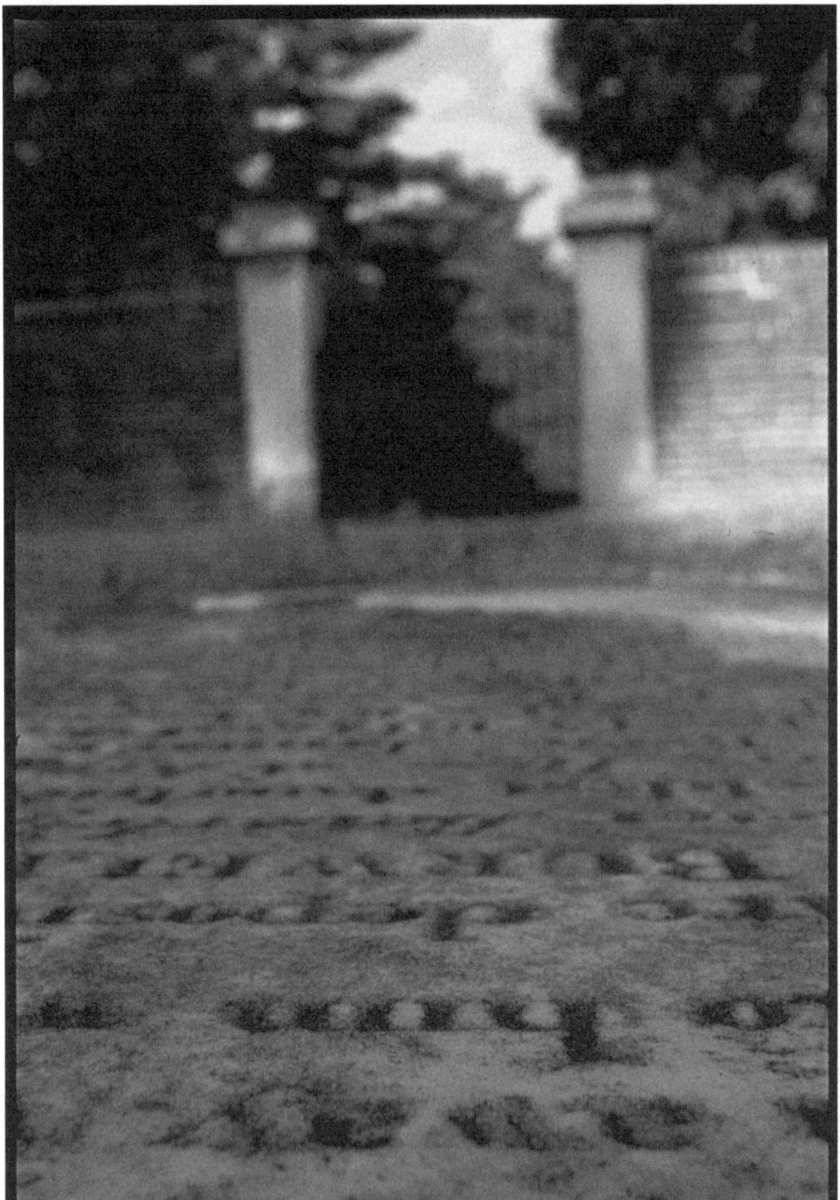

# Quetzal, Resplendent

Justin Bryant

***Belize travel journal, day 12***

The monkey is the first thing you see. He sits on a low branch, scraping at the moist bark of the tree with a curved fingernail. Bars of sunlight stream around his small frame and into the tall grass at your feet. The monkey—a black howler—looks up at you and stops scraping. Satisfied you mean him no harm, he puts his fingernail in his mouth and nibbles at the bark. The sun streams, he nibbles at the bark, and you watch him.

* * *

Colin Beal, thinker of practical matters: the meshing of cosmic gears were none of his concern. He smiled frequently, enjoyed excellent digestion, and every night fell quickly into eight hours of uninterrupted sleep. He read how-to books and biographies, watched action movies and the odd hockey game on TV, played golf every Friday afternoon, and listened to Top 40 radio. His friends considered him more level-headed than smart, and more friendly than level-headed.

He once saw an osprey pluck a fish from the Banana River and fly with it clutched in its talons. The fish didn't struggle. It flew with the osprey like a passenger. He thought it was strange. It occurred to him then, briefly, that there might be more intrigue and drama in the world than he had ever considered. He made a mental note to consider it later.

***Belize travel journal, day 17***

The black howler is neither a thinker nor an imbecile. He sees that on some nights half the moon is missing, and on others it is full, and it is not immediately clear if this affects him in any way. He scratches at the damp bark as you watch, and behind him, through the impossible jungle of geckos who lick their own eyes and birds with great beaks like cigars, the land steams and boils and grows to the sea, where only the salt beats it back. Look again at the howler. He moves away through the limbs without a backward glance, leaving you to stay or follow as you please.

* * *

Colin began looking for birds from his dock. He bought an Audubon guide to the birds of prey of North America. He read about ospreys and stood on his dock and waited to see more. He saw none the first afternoon, but within a week became familiar with several that perched regularly in the slash pines that grew from coquina rock along the river. He watched them dive for fish and was impressed by their high rate of success. He also saw pods of dolphins roll by the dock. When they surfaced and exhaled through their blowholes, it sounded as clear and distinct as if he were riding on their great gray backs.

***Belize travel journal, day 24***

There are paths and caverns in the jungle known only to the howler, and though you follow closely, you quickly become lost. Bipedal disadvantage: you're too tall and too bare to duck under the saw grass. What's worse is that your advanced thinking hinders you. The howler moves freely, while you consider options and strategies. So you walk upright but fall farther behind.

The mosquito clouds descend, the leeches grasp at your ankles, and the jungle asserts itself. Stay here for long and you'll become part of it: the creeping molds will grow up your legs, you'll inhale fungus spores and sprout tiny mushrooms under your tongue, you'll learn to live in the trees. You'll form calluses and eat grass, but it won't be an evolutionary regression. It will be advancement, for you will be adapting. Adaptability is the greatest measure of terrestrial competence.

* * *

Colin knew his birds. He named them, but knew better than to care about them. They were ospreys and could fly away forever any day, so he named them after the toady assistants and temps he'd entrusted to run his business.

He learned that the ospreys perched at the same time every afternoon, when the angle of the sun helped them see fish in the water. He also learned the routine of the local pods of dolphins. In the late afternoon, when the thunderstorms piled up above the central Florida landmass and tumbled east towards Merritt Island, spreading their icy anvils across Cocoa Beach, the dolphins returned from feeding in the green fleshiness of the ocean and passed by his dock, blowing what he liked to imagine were greetings as they rolled up the river.

One evening, the dolphins broke their ritual and lingered by the dock. Colin called to them. He dropped bait into the water, but they ignored it. He clapped and whistled, but they circled without approaching, then swam away towards the upriver lagoon where they spent their nights.

"Echo-location," Colin said, looking at the ospreys in the trees. "They can echo-locate, with sonar." The birds regarded him with jerky alertness. "And you guys can see in the dark, right?"

He watched the sunset from his dock, as he did every evening now. JoAnne often joined him, though not always, and not on this night. He liked to watch the sunset, and just recently it had reminded him of his Uncle Rick. When Colin was about ten, Rick told him, "Sunsets don't really start until the sun is gone. Watch the way the light catches the high clouds. That's the afterglow. Always wait for the afterglow."

Even then, Colin knew his Uncle Rick was regarded as his family's black sheep, having divorced twice and failing to establish a definite career. His status didn't seem to bother Rick, and it certainly didn't bother Colin. He assumed Rick was as happy as a man could be, so he listened to everything Rick said.

Colin sat on his dock and watched the sunset, watched the colors seep and fade from the clouds. He walked down the dock to the rocky shore, then closed his eyes and tried to find the way to his back door by memory and intuition.

***Belize travel journal, day 33***

What is happening to your senses, are they becoming more acute? Can you detect motion, sense heat, kill with your hands? Can you shed your skin, sleep with your eyes open, follow the moon? Have you found the howler? Can you hear the lizard grow?

You will have to.

* * *

JoAnne started going to the gym and then visiting her mother every afternoon—anything to get a little time away from the house, from Colin and his birds, Colin with the ruby-lensed binoculars hanging from his neck and a journal filled with the day's observations, cryptically and self-indulgently written to himself in the second person. She didn't begrudge him his new obsession—she found it charming and sweetly boyish, the way, for the first time since she had known him, he immersed himself in something purely recreational. But he'd taken to reading her his journal every day and describing everything that happened in the trees and river, and she just couldn't make herself care about birds.

Colin had long ago stopped going to the office, a move that instantly doubled his popularity there. Nobody wants the boss hanging around. He spent his mornings and evenings on the dock. In the afternoons he went to the library and read about tropical birds.

He asked JoAnne if she'd mind if he took a bird-watching trip. She said no. He asked her to come along, and she laughed and again said no. His travel agent arranged a ticket to Belize. Belize: toucans, parrots, jabiru storks as expansive as scaffolding, maybe even resplendent quetzals, if he was really lucky. He flew out three days later.

***Belize travel journal, day 39***

The Mayans knew this feeling, crouching in the prickly heat, sweating into the red earth. Waiting. They had the benefit of faith. You have none, nor have you a guide. The howler is no guide, no guru, and in any case, he has left you behind. You find toucans and parrots, watch them swoop and screech and beat the air, watch them drop and rise. You find spiders the size of your hand, trees buttressed into thin soil, ruined cities and temples. There is malaria, sweaty shaking and chills, and bad water or food that leads to convulsions in the bush. But the sickness passes and your journal entries grow longer, and the birds come and go, and you write.

* * *

Colin found toucans in the Cockscomb Basin, took a bus south into the Toldeo rainforests and sketched common parrots, shook with fever in Monkey River Town, ate fried plantains with salt, cut his feet walking barefoot. He crossed into Guatemala and stood at the feet of the Temple of the Jaguar at Tikal. Soldiers with AK-47s scolded him for giving coins to a homeless man. He talked with backpackers who smoked pot and bathed in Lake Atitlan. He rattled west on the bus, an old American school bus from Texas. The rainy season came. Bruised clouds rolled from the mountains every afternoon, rumbled, and fell open. He extended his return ticket once, then, when that date approached, had it open-ended. He crossed back into Belize, shortly before the roads became impassable. He settled in a small backpackers' lodge in Benque Viejo. The Mopan River, shallow and emerald, burbled past the village, past the Xunantunich Mayan ruins. Every evening he sat on top of the ruins. He watched the sun set across Benque, across the Guatemalan border a few miles away. He thought about the ospreys back in Merritt Island. He wrote in his journal from atop the ruins, just before the sudden coming of equatorial night. Sometimes he wrote about the birds he'd seen, sometimes about the villagers at the river, or the river itself, and sometimes he wrote letters to JoAnne. He'd mail the whole thing to her later.

***Belize travel journal, day 44***

Have you ever seen a sunset that doesn't really begin until long after the sun has gone? High, thin clouds catch the last rays and are illuminated, all the brighter since they stand against a darkened sky—have you seen it?

You found the black howler monkey, but he had nothing to say. This land here, it's not magic. It's just jungle—nothing so special. Vine and fern, lizards, colorful birds. It's a feast, but not a teacher. At least, not if you look at it as a teacher, because then all you'll see are the details—the scales, the bark, leathery bat wings, columns of ants, fallen coconuts, tangled sinew of growth. That's all—growth, biology. Hard science.

What you have to do is let your focus fade. Instead of sorting and compartmentalizing, just take it all in at once. Wait for the monkey to leave. Drop the binoculars, put down the journal. Watch the sunset, Colin.

Here comes the afterglow.

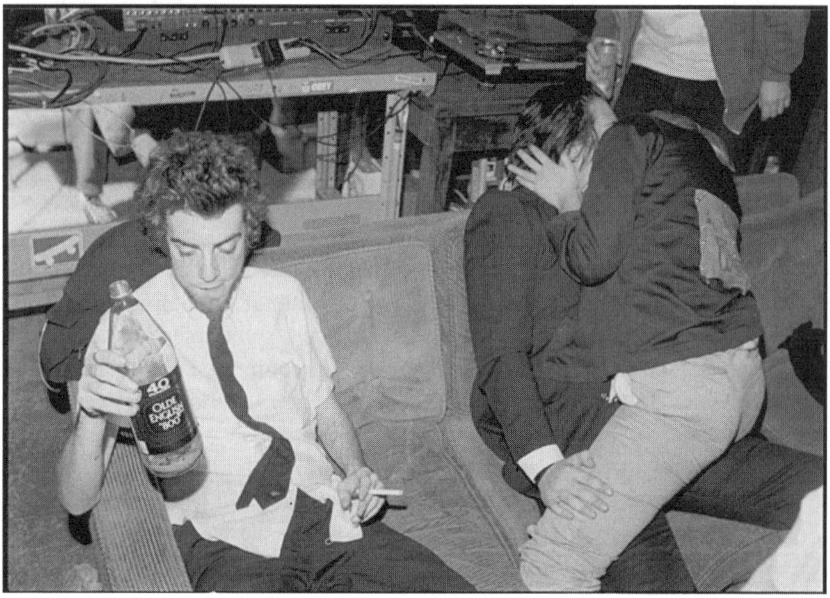
40
OLDE ENGLISH "800"

# frivolous, temporal, excusable

Travis Fristoe

The party was in full swing. Too loud to comprehend every word, but the intonations clear. Eric Dolphy's *Live in Europe* LP was playing a bit too obviously, listeners heeding the power invoked in his name. But if there's a place for being overt, it's a party, no? Clichés are based on real scenarios, right? These are the things you say at parties. Why go out at all if you're not going to meet it halfway?

Even Mark was attempting to be loud. The comments he usually only thought or mumbled to himself, jagged and biting things, he let fly to the entire room. We are young. We are having fun. What else should we be doing, sitting in our cluttered room and writing a story about the party? Not tonight. Overanalysis might let you safely grasp the tail of the beast, but you'll never taste the true victories. The faithless know only grape juice and crumbling wafers. Thus, we swallow and continue.

Young women look better at parties drinking red wine and laughing uniquely. Young men look better at parties against the wall in twos and threes, speaking only amongst themselves and staring like beggars. The Wu-Tang Clan sounds good at a party. Morrissey's solo albums do not. Names may change, but tone never does. Does the music adapt to you, or you to the tones? Is the DJ seamless (like the hand of God) or audacious (like an overeagersalesman)? Again, parties make you think such thoughts. Not going to parties makes you think worse things.

If the scenarios are a bit stock (leftover bags of Burrito Brothers chips; sleeveless black dresses with which to foil new tattoos; the way fluorescent light plays off hair gel; the nervous sway of wallflowers), can it not be forgiven? Are not the stereotypes here based on more successful scenes? Thus, when you put your mouth to the glass I can't help but think of kissing you. You will taste of wine still, a breathing embodiment of possibility. Turning grapes into wine, dark moments into sweeter memories. If such transformations are not possible at parties, why go? If you don't believe the wine will transform you, why would you drink it? Alchemy through sheer will!

We move cautiously between the cerebrally silent and the compellingly tangible. Mark thinks of how above these gatherings he is until Claire cuts her eyes at him. What significance such glances? How solipsistic and foolish his snide thoughts seem when there's the possibility of life so close? *Why do I always complicate these matters*, Mark reprimands himself. She looks at me, I look back. We smile. A biogenesis. Conversation and causality will carry us the rest of the way, he hopes.

Claire sees Mark with his nervous, bitten lips and thinks if this were a movie or story, then one of us would sweep the other away with the right comment. That is what we're waiting for, right? A suitable ending. Don't (basically) good people deserve (basically) happy endings? Friends and observers become anxious, eager to become the hands of fate themselves. Readers of the story become impatient. We have to wait enough in life, why can't art be tidier, concise as a kiss, revelatory as that first glance?

We are between records, a pivotal point in the evening. Some of the guests are leaving. Some have already left. The hostess, an overcompensating minor character named Kelly, laughs too loud and too long. Mr. Winks, the housecat, abruptly scratches a partygoer who's been petting him. The 2 A.M. alcohol deadline approaches—are we fortified? Sufficiently lubricated? Has another evening been pissed away with uncertainty? Oh, is it too late?

Claire, in fear of the too-late part, moves toward the door. If Mark wants to pursue, then he will have to physically follow. *He'll have to meet me at least halfway*, she thinks. *I can't wait all night and I can't do everything,* she thinks. This is the next understood stage. The stand-ins and extras bar the path to outside. Claire maneuvers calmly and methodically through them—hips and shoulders brushing, cups and bottles threatening to spill out.

The door is visible now, the cool air palpable. Even the night sky is teasingly visible, a velveteen shade of blue and black. Streetlights giving off haloes of focus. Or so it seems, as our characters approach the exit.

Mark, more scared of losing the tenuous thread, turns to his friend Pat and says, “All right—I’m out,” and moves toward the door without waiting for a reply or acknowledgment from Pat. Pat, accustomed to such outcries and leavings, waves to Mark’s turned and shrinking back. The cowlick Mark tries in vain to suppress quivers like a small antenna leading him towards the signal.

He has a rougher time making his way through the crowd. Partygoers crowd not just the walls and couches, but most of the unfurnitured space also. A clear path is not evident. He thinks someone is calling his name from across the room, but he doesn’t recognize the voice. How many Marks are there at this party? Surely, more than one. All his attention is going towards the figure of Claire and the back of her head, now half in the party and halfway out the door.

The sweat cools on Claire’s neck as she passes through the threshold. The bottom of her haircut appears to Mark like an arrow pointing down her spine. How fortunate to be born with such a hairline clean and clear as a stigmata. *No, not like a stigmata*, Mark thinks. *I don’t want to think about bleeding wounds from her neck. It’s more like a mole transformed into a beauty mark. What will I say to her when her head turns and I see her entire face?* There must be a word for these culminating hairs at the base of her head, but what is it? The moment is approaching, dead set and irrevocable.

So much setup for such fleeting action!

Prescient, Claire turns to look on the party from outside the warehouse. Their faces appear kinder from outside, their talk a gentle buzzing. All forgivable. And into this rare generous space, Mark steps.

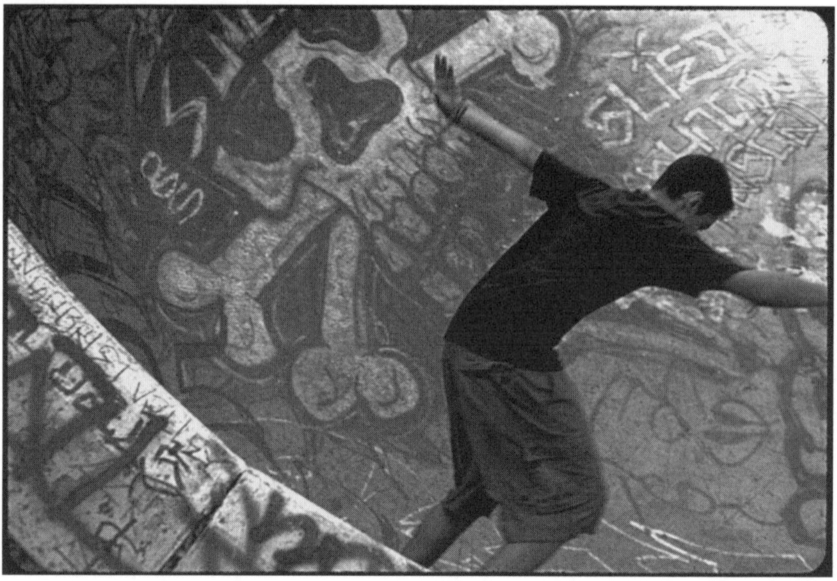

# Sid Harper and the Capitol of Doom

Sean Carswell

Sid looked out the window at the gathering mass of police cars, SWAT vans, fire trucks, ambulances, news crews, red-and-blue swirling lights, and lights glaring a fake TV yellow. Beyond it all, the first hints of dawn crept up the horizon. He examined the scene below him slowly and carefully until he was sure that the pizza guy wasn't anywhere in the crowd. I'm screwed, he thought.

He stepped back from the window. He walked over to a desk, lifted a bottle of whiskey, took a gulp, and set it back down. He sat in the chair behind the desk. It was a big leather chair. A chair that cost more than Sid made in a month. A congressman's chair. The whiskey had belonged to a congressman, too, but it wasn't expensive like the chair. Just a fifth of good ol' Jack Daniels. He lifted the bottle to his lips again, but before he could drink, the phone rang.

Sid snatched it up and screamed, "Where's my fucking pizza?" His own anger surprised him. It made him laugh at himself. He covered the mouthpiece so that the caller wouldn't hear him laughing.

"The pizza's coming. I promise," the caller said. "But you gotta give us something first."

Sid went ahead and took his slug of whiskey. He knew that the pizza wasn't on the way. He knew that the caller's promise meant nothing, all of the caller's promises meant nothing. Most of all, Sid knew that the standoff was over. He said, "I'll give you one hostage: the cleaning lady's skater boyfriend. He's pissing me off, anyway. But I want my fucking pie." Sid slammed down the phone before the caller could say anything.

He picked up the bottle of whiskey and the Cuban cigar that he'd found in another congressman's desk. He cut the end of the cigar, set the cutter on the desk, lit the cigar, and took a couple of puffs. He stood up and started for the front door.

It was that kid's fucking shirt, he thought. If not for that stupid fucking shirt, I might've made it through tonight.

* * *

Much earlier that night, Sid and his friend Bobby had gone to the Tallahassee skate park. The city kept the lights on at the skate park until eleven most nights, and Bobby and Sid would usually get there around ten and get in an hour of exercise after the heat of the day and before the lights went out. Like typical old skaters—guys who'd made it into their thirties and realized that a skateboard would never get them laid, no matter what tricks they pulled—they'd hang out by the bowl. The bowl was shaped like a swimming pool, basically, with a five-foot shallow end, a nine-foot deep end, and gradual transitions on the walls. Right next to the bowl was a bench, where typical old skaters caught their breath between runs.

By ten-thirty that night, Bobby and Sid were spending most of their time on that bench, talking about shit, watching the kids skate in the street part of the park, and occasionally taking a run in the bowl. And this was when the kid showed up.

He was a skinny kid, probably a freshman or sophomore at Florida State University, and he skated the bowl like it was a half-pipe: going only from one side of the bowl to the other, turning around, coming back, grinding the rail, pulling a few of the easier tricks. This didn't bother Sid. The kid skated a lot, taking more turns in the bowl than Bobby or Sid, but they were tired and this didn't bother them, either. But every time the kid's back was turned to them, they saw, in big black letters, the words, "I skate therefore I am."

"That shirt, Bobby," Sid said.

"What about it?"

"That fucking shirt."

"What about the shirt?"

"That fucking shirt is driving me batty."

"Shit," Bobby said, "you were batty long before that shirt came along." Bobby picked up his skateboard and walked over to the shallow end of the bowl. Right about the time Bobby got there, the kid tried a long grind that ended with him falling on his ass. He popped right back up, picked up his board, and ran out of the bowl. Bobby dropped in.

By the time Bobby finished his run, Sid's breakdown had begun.

The kid looked petrified. Sid was a scary-looking guy if you didn't know him. He was a tall guy, about ten pounds overweight, with his head shaved bald and sleeves tattooed up both his arms. And he had a way of looking at people when he talked to them: he'd stare, his forehead wrinkled and his eyebrows so low that they cast a shadow over his eyes. It was an expectant look. It was the look of a man who demanded that the next thing you say be the wisest, most important thing you've ever said. Or else. He gave the kid this look and said, "I know what it *says*. I want to know what it *means*."

"I skate therefore I am."

"I can read, dumbshit," Sid said. "I want you to explain to me what that statement means to you."

"Look, man, it's just a shirt," the kid said.

"Yes, it's just a shirt, but it's a shirt that you chose to purchase and wear and thereby spread the message of the shirt and I want to know what that message is."

The kid stared straight ahead, avoiding eye contact with anyone. He placed his hand on the bench and shifted all of his weight onto it, as if he were about to spring up and run away. Bobby, not noticing this, sat next to the kid, trapping the kid in his seat. Sid kept staring down at him. A long, silent moment passed.

"See, it's like this: I know I'm freaking out," Sid said. "This much is clear to me and it's becoming clear to you. But you see me and you think I'm a threat. And I am. I might just kick your ass for wearing that shirt. But that's not the point. Not yet. The point is this: you see me coming down on you and you hear my voice, so you assume I'm really here, getting mad about all this shit. But have you ever thought you saw something, then looked closer and realized it wasn't what you thought you saw? Have you ever thought you heard something, then listened closer and realized it wasn't what you thought you heard? Of course you have. So your vision and your hearing have betrayed you in the past. You can't trust them. So you can't know that I'm really here based on what you see and what you hear. And you only have three more senses. Maybe you think you can smell me, but Bobby's knee pads stink so fucking bad that there's no way any of us can smell anything else."

Bobby laughed at this. He shook his head, picked up his skateboard, and went for another run in the now-empty bowl.

The kid leaned on his hand again, ready to jump.

Sid kept up his rant. "So you can't trust your smell. And I haven't hit you yet, so you haven't felt me. And you damn sure haven't tasted me. And that's all you have." Sid counted out on his fingers. "Sight, hearing, smell, touch, and taste. Everything you know in life you learned through those five senses. And if you can't trust any of them, how do you know I'm here?" Sid paused. The kid didn't say anything. "It wasn't a rhetorical question. I'm asking. How do you know I'm really here? How do you know that your mind is not just playing tricks on you? Christ, does this shit really happen in the real world? Do people really lose their shit over a stupid ass t-shirt?" Sid paused again. The kid looked as confused as he was terrified, but he still didn't say anything. Sid said, "So my question to you is this: how do you know that this is really happening?"

"I dunno," the kid said.

"See, that's exactly it. You *don't* know. You don't know anything for sure. You could be a complete lunatic with a really good imagination. Right now, you could be sitting in a mental home somewhere, or just wandering the streets, homeless and lost and imagining that you're a twenty-year-old kid who's getting harassed at a skate park. You don't think that's the case, but no lunatic thinks he's a lunatic, right?

"And, besides that, your mind—when you're sleeping—has convinced you of all kinds of things that weren't really happening, right? Haven't you had dreams that seemed just as real as this moment right now? So how do you know that this isn't all just a dream? In fact, how do you know that you even exist at all?"

"Look, man, I just came here to skate," the kid said.

"No, that's not the right answer," Sid said. "The right answer is this: you *know* you exist because you *think* you exist, and you must *exist* to *think* you exist. In other words, your thought has to come from somewhere. It has to come from someone who exists, right? So, you think, therefore you exist. Or, as René Descartes said four hundred years ago, 'I think, therefore I am.' I think—comma—therefore I am.

"This is the basis for all western philosophy. This is the starting point for the scientific method. This is the birthplace of modern science. It's hard to believe, but you wouldn't have that skateboard or the technology to make it if Descartes hadn't said that.

"But 'I *skate* therefore I am'? No fucking comma? How the fuck does that make any sense at all?" Sid stared down at the kid. The kid squirmed a bit under the stare.

Bobby finished his run and sat next to the kid. "Get a grip, Sid," he said. "The bowl's open. Why don't you take a turn?"

Sid stood and pointed his tattooed arm at the kid. "Don't you go anywhere," he said. "I'm not through with you." Sid walked over to the bowl and dropped in. Bobby and the kid sat on the bench and watched Sid carve and grind and occasionally powerslide. In the bowl, Sid seemed remarkably calm. Serene, even. Then, he lost his board when he hit the metal coping too hard. The board flew out of the bowl and Sid slid down the shallow end on his knee pads. When the slide ended, he pulled himself together and climbed out of the bowl.

The kid took his turn. After he fell, Bobby took a turn. After all of that, the three of them ended up on the bench again. No one said a word until Sid said, "Just understand that Descartes proved that he existed, but that was all. He couldn't prove that this isn't all just a dream, that we're not all raving lunatics or hallucinating or making up this whole world in our minds to keep from dealing with some horrible truth. No one could prove that. Not George Berkeley. Not Benedict de Spinoza. Not even David Hume—though Hume came close to proving it, really close. Still, the point is that Descartes could only prove that we exist because we think we do. And from there, he asked, 'Well, what are we?' and realized that all we can say we are, without a shadow of a doubt, is a thinking thing. That's it. Not a human. Not a Floridian. Not a skater. Just a thinking thing."

Sid grabbed his board and ambled to the edge of the bowl. He propped the tail of the board on the edge, set his back foot on the tail, turned to the kid, and said, "Then you come around here wearing that stupid-ass shirt, and you're not even *thinking*. So what the fuck kind of thing are you?"

After the skate park closed, Bobby gave Sid a ride home. They were halfway to Sid's house before Bobby or Sid said anything. The two just rolled through the Tallahassee night, listening to tinny music claw its way out of Bobby's blown-out speakers. Finally, Bobby said, "Spoke to your dad lately?"

"No," Sid said. "Not for a few months. Why?"

"Because you're cracking up," Bobby said. "I figured your dad had something to do with it."

Sid looked at Bobby with that look that demanded Bobby say something wise. Bobby didn't say shit. Bobby stared ahead at the road with a look on his face that seemed to say, *You're a thinking thing. Figure it out.*

So Sid thought about it. He thought about his dad.

Sid's father was a philosophy professor with a fucked up sense of humor. When Sid was a kid, his father used to tell him to sit under a tree and eat a grain of rice a day and see if it led him to believe that all life was suffering. It took Sid fifteen years to get the joke, to realize that his name was a pun. Their family name was Harper. This was why Sid's father named him Sid. Sid Harper. As in Siddhartha. The Buddha. The originator of the grain-of-rice-a-day diet and the all-life-is-suffering notion. The name was all just Dr. Harper's way of making his son the butt of a bunch of jokes about eastern philosophy.

When Sid was in high school, Dr. Harper would make Sid read philosophy texts again and again until he could write his father's lectures for him. And Dr. Harper never used the lectures. Not once. But he was the academic equivalent of the Little League coach who makes his son cry with every strikeout. He rode and pushed Sid and threatened him through all the great minds of western civilization, and no matter how much Sid resisted, a lot of it stuck in his mind. Most of it did. He couldn't work a job without getting lost in meditations about Keirkegaard's master-and-slave relationships. He couldn't read crime novels without thinking of Neitzche's superman. He couldn't take heavy drugs without cornering some poor bastard and forcing him through a rant about the Rationalists.

It was a strange and painful childhood for Sid. One for which he could never find a support group or a self-help book. One which he was best to try to convince himself never existed. A childhood full of some actions that led to inevitable reactions. It was inevitable that he'd rebel against his father, and Sid did. Just like that kid who cries at every strikeout inevitably becomes a ballet dancer just to spite his dad, Sid found the ultimate way to become a three-foot-high flame, forever burning his father's ass. It took him several years to figure out how, but he found a way: he became a web programmer. But not just any web programmer. Sid was the guy behind the Florida State University football team web site. This tortured Dr. Harper to no end: to know that Sid *did* work for a university and *did* use his intelligence, but did it in the most meaningless way possible. It was even worse when, at the occasional family dinners, Sid would say things to his father like, "You know, for every student of yours who actually reads the Kant essays you assign, I bet there's a thousand students who read the pre-game injury report I posted today. I bet the ratio is actually more like one to ten thousand."

There were some other inevitable reactions, too. Like Sid's string of manual labor jobs before becoming a web programmer. Like the six years that Sid spent drunk and/or high. Like Sid breaking down at the skate park. Like everything that would follow in his breakdown.

This, Sid realized, was Bobby's point. "Psychotherapy comes easy for you, huh?" Sid said.

Bobby kept his eyes on the road and said, "I'm not trying to oversimplify things, here. I'm just saying that your dad's a cruel bastard and philosophy fucks with everyone. You combine the two, and, well, a breakdown at a skate park might occur."

What Bobby didn't say this time—though Bobby had said it dozens of times before—was, "Shit, Sid, after meeting your dad, I don't blame you for anything you do."

"It's more than that," Sid said.

"It always is."

Sid didn't explain and Bobby didn't try to pry an explanation out of him. They drove down West St. Augustine Street, past the university. Bobby took his eyes off the road to idly glance up at the state capitol building, looming ahead in the distance. Sid picked at the dirt underneath his fingernails. Bobby turned left on Macomb Street. Sid toyed with the thought of trying to talk Bobby into going to a bar, even though Sid knew Bobby hadn't had a drink in years. Even though Sid knew that all his memories of his drinking days had been romanticized by now. Sid had forgotten about all the problems of those days: the bills he could never pay and the diarrhea he'd get from drinking and all the college girls he never should've slept with and all the cavities he'd gotten from too many bourbon and cokes. He knew he'd forgotten all of that and only remembered those rare times when all his friends were out and none of the drama seemed too much and the future didn't seem to be such a wash.

But Sid thought about it more and he did remember the time when he saw Bobby naked, jumping on the trampoline at their friend's child's fifth birthday party. Sid remembered when he had to peel Bobby off the grass of the Zen Hair Salon on Tennessee Street, also, because Bobby was passed out drunk there at two-thirty on a Tuesday afternoon. He remembered the three days that Bobby mysteriously stunk like canned fish, and no one could explain why. So Sid kept his mouth shut and let Bobby turn left onto Pensacola Street and away from the bars.

Bobby took a quick right off of Pensacola Street and into Sid's driveway and parked. Sid took extra time collecting his gear. He slowly opened the door. He placed one foot on the dirt driveway. He pulled his elbow and knee pads out of his helmet, rearranged them, and stacked them back into the helmet again. He said, "I don't feel like going inside. It's like a wake in there."

But there was no bar that Bobby could go into and nothing to do now that the skate park had turned their lights off, so Sid went inside.

* * *

Sid's wife Elena and a group of her friends and ex-co-workers filled up the living room. There was a butt on every seat cushion and couch cushion in the room, and most of the floor space was covered, too. Sid waved at the crowd as he walked by, and headed into the kitchen.

The kitchen was fairly well full, too, but mostly cluttered with used up goods. Tortilla chip crumbs in a bowl, guacamole with that bruised-black crust forming on the edges, a dish of watery hummus, a vegetable plate with only the raw zucchini surviving. The counter was covered with empty bottles of imported beer and designer fruit drinks and sodas that Sid had never heard of. He walked over to the fridge, opened the door, and looked inside. His hand lingered over a bottle of brown ale for a full thirty seconds before he finally grabbed the beer.

In the living room, Elena's friends were talking about the downfall of the *Tallahassee Guardian*. Most of them worked for the *Guardian*, which was one of the longest running independent weeklies in the US, or at least it *had* been independent until it had been bought out a month earlier. The buyout meant that almost everyone in Sid's living room would be unemployed within a month. This was why they'd all gathered at Sid and Elena's: to discuss strategy, to bitch about the future, to heighten the importance of their lives in their own minds. Sid pulled out his key chain. He opened the beer from the bottle opener on the key chain, and sat at the kitchen table.

It was true that Sid didn't drink much anymore. It was also true that he didn't want to face the crowd in his living room until he'd had at least one drink. He sat at the kitchen table and eavesdropped.

"No one's gonna write about any of this shit anymore," one guy said. "It's like this new alarm system at the capitol. Have you guys heard about that?" A few people grunted in agreement. Someone prodded the guy to explain himself. "Yeah," the guy said, "they just installed an alarm system in the capitol that cost a *million* and a half dollars. There's no money in this state for public schools, and FSU can't get funding for summer classes, but there's a million and a half dollars for a new alarm in the capitol."

"What was wrong with the old alarm?" someone asked.

"What kind of alarm was it?" someone else asked.

"It's even worse than that," a woman said. Sid couldn't see into the living room from the kitchen, and he didn't know any of Elena's friends well enough to recognize their voices. He didn't even remember their names most of the time. But he did hear this one woman very clearly when she said, "A friend of mine helped install that alarm system. He told me that they didn't wire any of the screens in the building. He said that they wired the window frames and frames of the window screens, but if someone left a window unlocked, you could just cut the screen out and crawl into the capitol building."

"But they'd still have motion detectors inside, right?" the first guy asked.

"No," the woman said. "They can't have motion detectors or the night janitors would..."

"How was skating, Sid?"

Sid looked up to see Elena had come into the kitchen. She stood in front of him.

"Hey, honey," Sid said. "I stole one of your friend's beers."

Elena looked at the pile of empty bottles and the crusty appetizers and said, "Fair enough."

"Doesn't sound like this party is winding down," Sid said.

Elena shook her head. "You know how it is with revolutionaries," she said. "They never know when to go home."

"Well, Jesus, I don't know why you have to be supportive of all these fucks. Especially considering..." Sid stopped himself. Elena had been the first one fired after the *Guardian* was bought out. She didn't need to be reminded of this.

After a short silence, Elena shrugged and said, "Yep... yep."

Sid let the subject drop. He took a pull off his beer. "I lost my shit at the skate park," he said.

"Really? What happened?"

Sid looked up at Elena. Behind her shoulder, the old *Guardian* managing editor, Bill or Dave or something, walked into the kitchen. Sid nodded to him and said to Elena, "This kid was wearing a shirt that said, 'I skate therefore I am.' That fucking shirt damn near drove me off the edge."

"The shirt did?" BillorDave said. Elena shot him a look.

"It's like this," Sid said, and explained the situation to him—from Descartes down to the Tallahassee skate park. Elena half-listened to Sid's lecture, half-watched BillorDave nod along, half-watched Sid watching her as he talked.

When Sid's lecture was over, BillorDave said, "See, that's exactly why it's tragic—in principle, anyway—that the *Guardian* was bought out: if no one covers these things, do they exist? If no one says, 'Hey, there was a massive genocide in Rwanda,' then no one cares enough to help the people of Rwanda..."

"It doesn't work like that," Sid said. "Rwanda exists whether you write about it or not. The whole world exists, regardless of whether or not we try to intellectualize it away or ignore it in the press. It's still out there."

"But what I'm saying..." BillorDave started to say.

"I know what you're saying," Elena said. She'd seen enough of her friends get wrapped up in Sid's philosophical discussions. She knew all of Sid's arguments backwards and forwards. She made it clear time and again that she'd be happy if she never had to hear about another philosopher for as long as she lived. "Sid's right," she said. "It doesn't work like that."

"Just hear me out. Take the current situation in the Middle East..." BillorDave said.

Sid pounded the rest of his beer and said to Elena, "I'm gonna let you two discuss this while I step out for an hour or two."

This time, it was Sid who Elena shot a look at. "Where are you going?" she asked.

Sid picked his keys and wallet up from the kitchen table, stuck his wallet in his back pocket, hooked his wallet chain to a belt loop, and said, "Just to the store to pick up a snack or something."

Sid knew that the "or something" was a six-pack of beer. He skipped the snack, grabbed the six-pack, and walked a couple blocks up Pensacola to an abandoned building.

A few decades ago, the building had been a house. Then, a lawyer bought it and set up his office there. Then it was a small art gallery. Then it was an antique store. Then it was for sale for two or three years. Then they boarded up the windows. During Sid's heavy drinking days, the building was an art gallery, and the owners never minded if Sid sat on the porch late at night, drinking alone. When the antique store owners took over, they saw Sid's late night drinking as something they inherited with the place, and they probably minded, but they never said anything to Sid. And once they left, no one was around enough to care.

Sid hadn't been back to the abandoned porch in over a year, but now that he had a sixer and needed a place to be alone, the porch seemed perfect. So he sat there and drank a beer and thought and drank another beer and thought some more.

He thought about what BillorDave was trying to say: that people act as if things don't exist simply because people don't see these things existing. Like so many kids closing their eyes at danger instead of fighting or running away. He tried to look at things from BillorDave's perspective—a managing editor's perspective—and figured that BillorDave *had* to feel that way. He had to believe that information made things exist, that independent weekly newspapers pried those little kids' eyes open and forced them to fight or flee. BillorDave had to believe this or what he did every day was pointless.

Elena had felt this way, too. That's why she'd started at the *Guardian* in the first place. Elena, who'd been drunk all those years with Sid. Elena who'd spent half her afternoons from April to October getting high and following every pitch of every Chicago Cubs game; who'd spend four nights a week in an upscale bar north of town, up by the country club, fixing martinis and chatting up rich white men and doing shots when no one was looking just to make it through her shift; who'd spend the other three nights a week blowing her tip money in other bars where she knew all the bartenders and every second round came with a free shot of Goldschlagger. This same Elena who sobered up and took a few journalism courses and poured all the energy that she'd once spent partying into writing about politics, researching every move of US foreign policy, following every bomb dropped and every small country invaded just like she'd followed the Cubs' box scores. She read books by liberal professors from the northeast and she studied documents she got through the Freedom of Information Act and she went to nearly every protest at the capitol steps and she wore out the plastic on three library cards just to keep up with US troop movements abroad. And just like a true Cubs fan, Elena always rooted for the underdogs, the small countries, hoping against hope that they'd be able to compete in the World Series. That they'd, just once, have a chance. This is why, when the *Guardian* was bought out, Elena was the first to go.

So Sid sat in the shadows of the abandoned porch and thought about this. He looked up at the capitol building and wondered if any of this stuff was worth it. He wondered if it was worth it for Elena to sober up at all; if sobering up and straightening out her life was, at its core, just another way of dumping all her time into a new, self-destructive obsession. He wondered if she was wondering these same things and if it helped her to have all the old *Guardian* folks over to the house for some kind of self-pitying group therapy. He wondered if she'd listened to anything BillorDave said about countries not existing because we don't read about them in the news, or if her week away from the paper had given her enough distance to realize how self-absorbed that thinking was.

Sid cracked open his third beer and explained it out loud to himself, because there was no one else there to listen. He explained that questioning your very existence was important—despite the fact that Sid wished that his father had never put him through all of this—

because it gave you a reference point, a point of perspective. As long as you could question your own existence and the existence of things around you; as long as you could make even a small part of your mind accept the possibility that you're all alone in a void, fooling yourself into believing that a whole world exists solely so that the emptiness doesn't drive you mad; as long as you could believe this, you would be immune to most belief systems. Because it's very difficult to believe in any abstract like a god or a government if you can't fully buy the fact that the chair you're sitting on isn't just a figment of your imagination. "Or, to put it another way, BillorDave," Sid said to the shadows, "only when you learn to question every little detail of your life will you be able to find meaning and make sense of deeper issues."

Sid went on to explain these concepts to Elena and Bobby, or at least to the shadows where Elena or Bobby would've sat if either of them were there with him. He thought and talked to himself and explained a lot of things. He drank a fourth beer and then a fifth. He looked out from the shadows at the moon dangling up above the capitol, at the empty streets of downtown, at the backside of the state Supreme Court to his right and the backside of the Civic Center to his left. When Sid cracked his sixth beer, he even invited the idea of his father to sit in the shadows with him, and explained the downfalls of sobering up and questioning everything and looking for meaning. He explained that to be focused on any one thing to the point of obsession—whether that one thing you were obsessed with was drugs or alcohol or US foreign policy or buying a new house or losing weight—was probably better than to waste your time searching for deeper answers. It was less confusing to just obsess. Healthier emotionally. "Think of the beauty inherent in believing it matters that the state installed a new security system," Sid said to the idea of his father.

"It's all useless information," the idea of Sid's father said. "If you don't do something about it, it's just trivia."

Sid drained the last of his sixth beer. He looked at his watch. It was seven minutes past two o'clock. "Well, then, let's use this information," he said to no one.

* * *

If it had been seven minutes before two o'clock instead of seven minutes after two, Sid probably would've stumbled around the corner, grabbed a tall boy of some cheap beer, and walked home harmlessly. As it was, the state had mandated that beer sales must end by two A.M., and with the steady stream of alcohol drying up, and with no more skate park, and with a living room full of downtrodden revolutionaries, and with a bunch of friends who'd sobered up for their own good, Sid had nothing left to do but stumble up to the state capitol and have a look.

He passed no one on his four-block walk up to the capitol. Not one single car rode down Pensacola Street. The whole little city was empty.

Sid approached the capitol from the south side. He walked up to the first window he saw, but it was clearly locked, so he went to the next window. Locked. And the next window, and the next. As he got closer to the front of the building, the landscaping took over. One window looked to be cracked open, but it was behind a thick bush. A gardenia plant. Sid climbed over the plant, tramping down weaker branches, and looked more closely at the window. Nope. Locked, too. Sid continued down the south side of the building, looking at windows and naming the landscape shrubs. Gardenia. Geranium. A crape myrtle coming in nicely on the lawn over there. Bougainvillea a few months shy of blooming. And so on. Sid hadn't thought about it much lately, but somehow, being drunk and trying to break into the state capitol reminded him of his days working for a landscaper. "Yeah," Sid said out loud to no one, "landscapers always have the best weed. I wish I had a landscaper with me right now." Sid smiled at the thought and saw another thick gardenia and another window that might just be cracked open. As he climbed over the plant and looked more closely, he saw that this window was, indeed, unlocked. The slightest breath of air floated between the bottom of the window and the top of the sill. "Well, here we go."

Sid took his keys out of his pocket and dragged his house key down the screen until the screen tore. He slid his fingers in the tear and pulled the screen apart until he had an opening about twelve inches long. He paused and listened. No sounds. No bells. No whistles. He stuck his right hand through the hole in the screen, placed his palm flat on the glass windowpane, and pushed up. The window slid open all the way. Sid stuck his head through the tear in the screen and listened. No honks. No beeps. No urban techno chorus of electronic screams. How about that? he thought. That *Guardian* girl was right. This million-point-five alarm system is no match for a drunken web programmer and a set of keys.

Sid tore the screen so that one long rip stretched from the top of the screen's frame to the bottom of the screen's frame. "Just like crawling out of the womb," Sid said to himself, and crawled through the long, vertical hole.

Sid had climbed into some kind of waiting room. He left it, and walked down the hallway and into the main lobby. No lights were on anywhere. No night janitors. Still no alarms going off. Sid headed for the elevators. His congressman worked on the eighth floor. Sid figured he'd pay the congressman a visit. They'd talk things over. Sid would make sure that the old boy was burning the midnight oil to earn the pay raise that all the congressmen had just given themselves.

Somewhere between the third and fourth floor, Sid realized that this was no joke. This was no philosophical exercise in the proof that politics and government existed. This was him *really* breaking into the capitol building of the state of Florida.

Somewhere between the six and seventh floor, he realized that he could either run out of the building and forget the whole thing and hope that no one came after him, or he could try to make something out of this situation he was in. *Carpe diem*, as his father would say. *Take this chicken and fuck it*, as his old landscaping boss used to say. So Sid grabbed the chicken by the wings and undid the zipper on his shorts—metaphorically speaking, of course.

Sid's first thought was to do something with the computer system. It was his field of expertise. He could download a virus and corrupt the entire network. But no, he decided, that would just be pointless destruction. The state would just buy more computers. They'd spend way too much money on them. Some poor fucking school would just lose more funding to pay for it. Sid thought about erasing the hard drive of his congressman's computer, erasing all the electronic files, all the congressman's work, all of his books, everything. But that would just fuck the congressman's secretary, Sid figured.

He walked into his congressman's secretary's office and booted up her computer. Something will come to me, he told himself. A brilliant plan is just under my top layer of consciousness, waiting to pop up, he told himself. I really should have planned this better, he told himself.

*An email!* he decided. He could get into the computer system, tap into the various senators' and congressmen's email databases, and mass email the constituency something about how politicians are just whores for lobbyists. Something about how the state was a shill for big business. Something about... shit, something that would be *news* to people. Damn. He should've planned this better.

The *Guardian* crew would know what to say. Sid thought about calling them, telling them that he'd broken into the state capitol and wanted to mass email the constituency about the sorry state of government, to tell them something they *didn't* know. Sid looked at the telephone. He gently tapped his index finger on the mouse. He let go of the mouse and picked up a paper clip and bent it into a weird shape and twisted it between his fingers. "Oh, goddamn it," he said out loud, shutting down the computer.

For the next hour, Sid wandered the halls of the capitol building, trying to think of something to do. He found a bottle of whiskey in a seventh floor office. He found some Cuban cigars on the twelfth floor. He rode the elevator all the way up to the twenty-second floor and looked out the windows at all of Tallahassee, sleeping below him. Still, not one creative thought crept into his mind. He decided that the best thing for him to do was to just leave. No one would know he'd broken in, anyway. Even if they did know that someone had broken in, they wouldn't investigate it, since nothing had been touched but a cigar and a bottle of Jack.

Sid took the express elevator down to the lobby. He stepped out into the great marble foyer. On his way to the window to crawl back out, he paused, took a shot of Jack, and said out loud, "Goddamn it. I'm fucking this chicken here."

He turned around and took the slow elevator back to the eighth floor. He sat back down at the congressman's secretary's desk. He grabbed a pad of paper and a pencil, made a quick list, picked up the telephone, and dialed the Tallahassee Police Department.

When an officer answered the phone, Sid said, "This is Sid Harper. I've taken the state capitol building hostage. I want to speak to someone who's prepared to meet my list of demands."

"Who is this?" the officer said.

"Sid Harper. I told you that already."

"What are you trying to pull? Is this a crank call?"

"You got caller ID, motherfucker?" Sid said. "Does this sound like a motherfucking crank call?"

There was a pause on the other end of the line. Presumably, the police officer checked his caller ID and saw that the call was coming from a congressman's line. The cop said, "Please hold while I transfer you."

Sid scratched the stubble on his face. He scratched the stubble on his head. His beard stubble was longer than his head stubble. It didn't make sense. A voice on the other end of the phone said, "Hello."

"Listen up," Sid said. "You got a pencil?"

"Calm down. Let's talk..."

"Fuck you. Do you know what's going on here? Do you know if

there are any hostages? Do you have any idea how serious this situation is? Now grab a motherfucking pencil and listen." Sid paused. He covered the mouthpiece of the phone with one hand. With his other hand, he lifted the bottle of whiskey to his lips. The whiskey wasn't really to steel his nerves. It was more to help him keep a straight face. All this screaming and making demands was cracking him up inside. *Or no*, he could almost hear Bobby say, *you were cracked up inside long before this*. "You ready to write?"

"Yes. Go ahead," the cop said.

"That's what I'm talking about," Sid said. "Now here's what I want: first, you got my phone number, right?"

"We've got the number to the congressman's office, where we know you are."

"Okay then, I want you to have three people call me. I want to speak to Jello Biafra..."

"Who?"

"Don't fuck with me. Just write. I want to speak with Jello Biafra, Ice Cube, and Timothy Leary."

"Timothy Leary is dead," the cop said.

"Didn't I just tell you not to fuck with me? Do you have any idea how volatile this situation is? Do you have any idea what I could do to this capitol building? Now listen, I want to speak to Jello Biafra, Ice Cube, and Timothy Leary. I want a CNN news crew outside. I've got some things to say. I want them to report it. And I'm hungry. I want a twenty-inch Gumby's pizza with extra jalapeños on the side..."

"Gumby's closes at two," the cop said.

"They're open all night, jackass. Now write: a twenty-inch pizza with jalapeños on the side. On the side. Got that. I want a six-pack of Asahi Dry to go with my pizza. I want..." Sid paused. From the outside, he could hear sirens. He knew the police station was close by, but he didn't expect the police to respond that quickly. "Are you sending cops here already?" Sid asked. "Don't you have any keggers for them to bust? Shouldn't they be waiting outside the Whataburger right now, giving drunk tests to anyone who goes through the drive-thru? Jesus Christ. I want you to understand that it would *not* be advisable for them to enter this building. Do you understand that?" Sid paused. He rubbed his head stubble again. He smiled to himself, then forced the smile back down with a taste of whiskey. "And, while we're at it, I want six hundred and sixty-six donuts for all the cops who are assembled outside. Krispy Kreme donuts. None of that Dunkin' Donuts crap. Only the best for our men in blue, right? You got all that?"

The cop read the list back to Sid. "Is that all?" the cop asked.

"That's it."

"Don't you want a helicopter to the airport? A flight out of the country? Anything like that?"

Damn, Sid thought. Those would be good things. I should've written that down. He said to the cop, "Nope. You have my demands."

Sid hung up the phone. He looked back over his list of demands and laughed. "Okay," he told himself. "I've got a soapbox that the world can hear me from. I better think of something to say."

* * *

Things to say didn't come easy for Sid. He paced the secretary's office. He glanced at the windows and made sure that he wasn't visible from them, that no sniper could take a shot at him. He thought of everything he would want to say, digging deep to find something that wasn't obvious to everyone. Because he was in the capitol building, whatever he said should be political, he decided. But he wasn't that political of a guy. He only knew the things that everyone knew: war is a bad idea; the US shouldn't be such a bully with its military; politicians are corrupt; schools are suffering; we should have a national health care system; on and on and on. It was all too obvious to mention.

He wished that Elena were there to help him. She'd know what to say. She'd actually done something with her sobriety. She'd redirected her energies. She believed that the same forces that led her to destroy herself could be turned around and used to make the world a better place. This belief had gotten her fired from her job, sure, but it had gotten her the job in the first place. It had given her a voice and people to listen, and she didn't have to break into the fucking state capitol building to have her voice heard.

Suddenly, Sid wanted very badly to be home in bed, to lie next to Elena and hear her breathe and feel the rise and fall of her chest as she slept. He decided to call her.

Elena picked up the phone on the first ring. "I fucked up," Sid told her.

"You sure as hell did," Elena said.

"I don't know what I'm gonna do."

Elena paused. Sid could hear her breathe. He could hear the television news on in the background. He didn't say anything. Just waited for her to talk. Finally, she said, "I know what you're gonna do.

You're gonna hang up this phone. You're gonna talk to the guy from CNN, and you're gonna say what you have to say. Then you're gonna give yourself up. I'll do my best to bail you out in the morning."

Sid wiped his sweaty palm dry on the leg of his pants. "You're right," he said. He felt the Cuban cigar in his pocket. He pulled the cigar out and twirled it in his fingers. When the next pause lasted into discomfort, Sid said, "You got any more advice for me?"

"Don't use any profanity," Elena said. "It just gives them an excuse to bleep out your words."

After the call to Elena, Sid knew exactly what to say from his soapbox. He organized his thoughts, took notes, and practiced his speech a few times. It was all clear and concise and made perfect sense. He was ready.

It didn't matter.

CNN never interviewed him. Jello Biafra never called. Ice Cube never called. Timothy Leary really was dead. The cops never got their donuts. The pizza guy didn't show. Sid never got his six-pack of Asahi Dry. After a while, the shots of Jack Daniels tore at his throat, and he had to keep running to the water fountain in the hall for a chaser. The jig was up.

Sid paced the floor of the congressman's secretary's office one more time, this time trying to figure out how to leave the building without getting shot. He walked over to the window, even though he felt confident that snipers were outside and that everyone knew he was on the eighth floor, in his congressman's office. He saw the lights of cop cars and emergency crews and news vans. He saw the cameras focused on talking heads reporting the situation without once calling Sid and asking what the situation was. He saw that the pizza guy wasn't coming. The phone rang.

Here goes, Sid thought. He screamed at the cop—the hostage negotiator—and offered to release one hostage: the cleaning lady's skater boyfriend.

Of course, there was no cleaning lady. There were no hostages. There was only Sid, with his shaved head and his gnarly tattooed arms and his black t-shirt and his plaid shorts, hoping the cops thought he was the "skater boyfriend" and therefore didn't shoot. He picked up his bottle of Jack. He cut the end of his cigar and lit it. He took the elevator back down to the lobby.

A minute later, he walked out into the light of the rising sun.

* * *

That morning, the Tallahassee newspaper ran a picture of Sid—the Capitol Kidnapper, they called him—walking down the capitol steps, with a bottle of whiskey and a big cigar. The newspapers referred to him as a "skinhead in his underwear", though he was no skinhead, and though what they referred to as "underwear" were really just a pair of plaid bermuda shorts. The newspaper printed a copy of his list of demands, written out in a child's handwriting, as if Sid had written and faxed the list. Three separate articles ran on the Capitol Kidnapper. All three of them claimed that his motive was "to speak his mind with the world listening."

That morning, local television stations covered the story of the "Siege of the State Capitol." They showed Sid walking down the steps. They ran the footage in slow motion to make Sid look more menacing. More stylized. Less drunk. They reported his demands and added a few demands and said, "This confused local man was simply looking for a soapbox from which to speak his mind." Neither the television news nor the newspapers acknowledged the fact that, all night, Sid never said anything to anyone in the press. Not one word.

That morning, the writers and editors at the *Tallahassee Guardian* started work on their "All Hail Sid Harper" issue. For one week, Sid would be a hero to anyone who read the weekly. For one last issue, the *Guardian* would spark a little controversy before becoming weekly fluff published solely for the sake of local advertisers.

And that morning, Elena drove to the other end of Pensacola Street to try to bail her husband out of jail, only to be told that Sid had been declared mentally unstable to stand trial, and he was in the process of being transferred to the state mental hospital in Chattahoochee. He would not be allowed visitors.

* * *

That morning, Sid was taken to the Tallahassee city jail. Instead of sticking him in a holding cell, the arresting officers brought him into what looked like a conference room. A state psychologist sat in the room, waiting for Sid. The interview lasted less than two minutes.

The psychologist said, "Your exit from the capitol building was interesting. I understand that you claimed to be," the psychologist glanced at the paper in front of him, "'the cleaning lady's skater boyfriend.' It's as if you feel like you're both hostage and kidnapper?" The psychologist paused again. "Have you ever been diagnosed as a schizophrenic before?"

Sid tried to explain that he didn't feel like he was a hostage. He had just pretended to be a hostage because he believed the police were less likely to shoot a hostage than they were to shoot him.

The psychologist asked Sid where this paranoia came from.

Sid explained that he wasn't being paranoid; that it was perfectly reasonable based on what he knew about police behavior to expect the cops to shoot at him when he walked out of the state capitol building.

The psychologist asked Sid how long Sid had had these delusions of grandeur.

Sid saw where this interview was going, so he simply stopped talking.

Within five minutes, the psychologist delivered his report. He claimed that Sid was a "paranoid schizophrenic with delusions of grandeur and a propensity to slip into a state of catatonia." Sid was quickly shipped off to the Florida State Hospital in Chattahoochee.

* * *

The first month at Chattahoochee was a tough one. Sid was placed in the minimum security ward, which was mostly prisoners like himself, but a few of the extra beds were taken up by voluntary patients. Sid spoke to no doctors and had very little contact with anyone except the occasional orderly and the nurses who checked to see if he was taking his meds—which he never did. He watched a lot of out-of-focus daytime television. He read a few out-of-date magazines on gardening, hunting, and cars. He spent a lot of time in his room, doing push ups and trying to play solitaire.

The toughest thing Sid had to deal with was his eyesight. After a couple of days, he couldn't stand to keep his contact lenses in his eyes any more. They were dirty and burned his eyes, but he had no way to store or clean them. In a fit of frustration, he pulled out his contacts and threw them away. It took two and a half weeks for him to convince an administrator that he couldn't see without glasses, and he needed an optometrist to help him out. After another week of Sid bouncing around blurry rooms, the state issued Sid a pair of bulky plastic glasses. At least he could see normally again.

Also during that first month—Sid found out much later—Elena tried to visit Sid on six different occasions, each time driving the hour and a half down I-10 with some different type of documentation proving that she and Sid were married and that the state hospital couldn't legally bar her from visiting Sid. On Elena's seventh visit, an observant hospital guard noticed that the marriage certificate had been notarized the day before the ceremony, and that, he said, nullified the contract. Sid and Elena were no longer married, according to the hospital guard. Elena's lawyer told her that the guard was full of shit, but it didn't matter. They were never going to let her see Sid, no matter what.

The second month at Chattahoochee, things started looking up. Sid finally got an appointment with a doctor. Well, an intern, but a woman who would be a doctor in a few months. Dr. Annette Pawlicki. Annette.

Annette was a student from the University of Chicago, finishing up her degree at Chattahoochee. She'd just moved to the small Florida town and was having some trouble adjusting. Sid and Annette chatted about this during their first interview. They talked about what she'd studied, about the research projects she'd worked on, and about the Ohio factory town she'd grown up in. After about twenty minutes of this, Annette said, "You seem like the most normal person I've met since I moved to Florida. Why are you here?"

"I got drunk and broke into the state capitol building," Sid said.

Annette opened up Sid's file. She glanced at a few lines. "Would this be the 'delusions of grandeur'?"

"No, I really did it," Sid said. "It wasn't that grand." Sid took a second to rub the now inch-long hair on top of his head. He added, "It was probably deluded, but definitely not grand."

Annette needed some convincing. She was new at the practice of psychotherapy. Things certainly didn't come as easily for her at the state hospital in Chattahoochee as they did for Bobby at the skate park in Tallahassee. Sid didn't spend the time convincing her. Instead, he gave her his home phone number. "Call my wife, Elena," Sid said. "She'll back me up."

The next visit went much more smoothly. Annette had done some research on the "Capitol Kidnapper." She told Sid that it had been hard to find anything about him, that there was almost no coverage of his "siege," and that no one in the hospital had anything to say about it. Finally, she resorted to asking her next-door neighbor if he'd heard anything about Sid. The neighbor had. In fact, he'd kept the newspaper report because the list of demands, particularly the 666 donuts, cracked him up. So anyway, Annette apologized to Sid for not believing him and said, "Weird. I watch the news and read all the time. I wonder why I never heard about this."

"I wonder why," Sid said.

Annette and Sid talked a lot about the break-in and the breakdown that led up to it. Sid explained all about the skate park and the "I skate therefore I am" t-shirt, and his father making him read all kinds of philosophy as a kid and how that fucked with him, and his years of drinking, and his occasional relapses into drunkenness that were mostly harmless and always short-lived, but, as he'd learned, could potentially go very awry. Sid also talked a lot about Elena and the *Guardian* and about all the petty tyrannies that wore away at him.

It took a few sessions. Annette didn't make any evaluations. She let Sid do most of the talking during most of the sessions and basically just repeated back to Sid whatever he said. During some sessions, Annette would do a lot of the talking. She'd often talk about herself, her schooling, the long-distance relationship she was in, her difficulty adjusting to small town life in Chattahoochee. Occasionally, she'd tell Sid that he was her only friend in North Florida.

They talked a lot about philosophy and psychology, too. Sid recommended essays and books. Annette brought in psychology journals and books for Sid to read. Sid read Carl Rogers's *On Becoming a Person* and came to understand Annette's style of therapy. He thanked her for loaning him the book. "I never loan these to anyone," she said, "because people are so bad about returning my books. But I always know where to find you."

On the third month, Sid convinced Annette to read a book about the Louisiana governor, Huey Long. The next week, he got her to pick up a book on the assassination of Martin Luther King, Jr. When Annette didn't make the connection between the two books, Sid helped her out. He redirected her to the pages that discussed Long's wrongful commitment to a mental institution in one book, and then he redirected her to the pages in the other book that discussed Grace Stephens—the woman who saw that the man fleeing the murder scene was definitely *not* convicted assassin James Earl Ray—and the twenty years she'd spent in a mental institution, despite psychologists' protests that she did not belong there. "Are you following me?" Sid asked.

Annette agreed that she did understand the point that Sid was making. "Both people were sane and committed to mental institutions so that they wouldn't cause any embarrassment politically," Annette repeated. "I see what you're saying." Then again, she said "I see what you're saying" about everything Sid said. It was the Carl Rogers way of going about things.

Later in that session, Sid said to her, "Sometimes I can feel a person's presence, and it makes me feel more comfortable. Like, when you pull into the parking lot of the hospital, I can feel you there. Like, sometimes I get these feelings that my friends are driving by on the highway that runs in front of the hospital. Does that make sense to you?"

Annette broke from her usual MO and said, "No, Sid. That makes no sense to me."

Sid didn't explain. He said, "I know I can't have visitors, but if you could tell my wife that I could feel her presence... If you could just call her and ask her to drive by the hospital... To stop the car on the side of the road and let me feel her presence..."

"I'm not following you, Sid."

Sid spoke slowly, deliberately. "If you could call my wife and ask her to drive to Chattahoochee and let me feel her presence..."

"I'm still not following you."

"Listen closely. I want you to call my wife and ask her to drive to Chattahoochee and pull her car off the highway on the other side of the woods from the hospital and to wait there. Preferably about two o'clock in the morning on this coming Wednesday. That way I can feel her presence..."

"I don't know what you mean, 'feel her presence'."

"Goddamn it," Sid said, more damning himself than damning Annette. "I'm trying to be sly and it's not working here, Annette. I'm gonna just come right out and say it: I'm gonna fucking rot here in this mental institution for the rest of my life, just like Grace Stephens, if I don't escape now. I can get out of here pretty easily, but I need a ride out of town. I need someone to call my wife and tell her to drive up here and wait by the side of the road at two o'clock in the morning this coming Wednesday."

Annette looked incredulous.

Sid looked at her as if he expected the next thing she said to be the most perfect thing she'd ever said. It was. She said, "I see. You want to *feel her presence*."

* * *

Sid had no trouble breaking out of the hospital. He didn't really even have to break anything. He just stole a pair of clothes from one of the sleeping voluntary patients' dresser drawers, put on the clothes, took a back stairway to the first floor, jimmied the door into one of the psychologists' offices, and climbed out the window.

He walked across the grounds behind the hospital, climbed the ten-foot chain link fence, and took off running through the woods. She'll be there, he told himself. I can trust Annette. I can trust Elena. It's going to happen. I'm free already.

Sid ran through the thick brush, scraping his legs on palmettos, jumping over cypress roots, dodging the southern pines. In the distance, cars ran down Highway 90.

Sid ran hard and fast for five minutes, aiming straight for the sound of the highway. Pretty soon, he could see glimpses of the headlights through the trees. He ran closer. In the distance, he could see what he thought was the shadow of a car pulled off to the side of the highway. He felt certain that it was Elena. Sure, his eyesight had betrayed him in the past. Sure, he'd seen things that turned out to be something else on closer inspection, but that shadow *was* Elena's car. He just *knew* it. He picked up his pace and ran for the highway and jumped and dodged and slid on wet spanish moss. His toe snagged on the root of a live oak. He flew face first into the dirt and weeds and a stand of ferns. His bulky plastic glasses flew further in front of him.

He got up on his knees and crawled around, looking for his glasses. Everything was dark and blurry. What once seemed to be trees were now just fuzzy shadows. Red and yellow lights from the highway were too far away to be anything. If there was any moon in the sky that night, it wasn't helping at all. He now just had a whole lot of darkness and the sound of the cars on the highway.

Half of Sid wanted to keep running for it. Fuck the glasses. Fuck his eyesight. Fuck it all. Elena would bring contacts for him. Of course she would. He could find his way through the forest without the glasses. The sounds would carry him. He'd just walk slowly and feel his way out. He could do it.

Sid stood and took two steps towards the highway. Everything was dark and wet and sounds echoed off the trees. No, no, he told himself. Fuck this. I need to see.

He dropped back down to his knees and crawled around the forest floor, feeling for his bulky glasses. He ran his fingers over dew and roots and weeds, but no glasses. He felt like he was replaying his frustrations from the capitol building, reliving that lost feeling that everything was fucked and he couldn't see to get out of it. He crawled and searched and dug through the ferns and couldn't put his hands on his glasses anywhere. He felt like a clown. A goddamn, fucking clown. A fucking laughingstock on an ass-backwards escape attempt.

But no, it was more than that. It was more than the breakdown and what he wanted to say to the press and what he never talked to Annette about. It was this void. This void that he'd slipped back into. This feeling of being completely lost. Not lost in the forest, but lost. Not blind without his glasses, but blind. Not groping for his glasses, but groping for something more tangible to hang on to. It was this big empty hole that he felt in the middle of this big, empty North Florida forest. This big empty hole that he felt like everyone felt. The hole that they'd all tried to fill with so much booze. The hole they tried to cauterize with smoke. The hole that just got bigger with sobriety. The hole that Bobby tried to fill with skateboarding and that Elena tried to fill with the *Guardian* and that Annette filled with Rogerian psychology and that Dr. Harper filled with Kant and that Sid never felt like he could fill. It was this feeling of being in the forest with everything fuzzy and blurred around him and closing in on him. This groping. This remote danger. This sense that he had to hurry. Or at least he was coming to a point where he'd have to hurry, where a series of ends were near. "Aw, fuck," he said to no one.

Sid's hands flailed in front of him, swooshing through pine needles and fallen leaves and small weeds and pine saplings. He crawled in circles, panicked. He searched so frantically that he couldn't hear the cars on the freeway and he couldn't hear the footsteps coming towards him. In fact, he didn't hear anything until he saw someone standing right in front of him. He winced. I'm fucked, he thought. They know I ran, he thought. They caught me, again, he thought.

Then, the someone standing in front of him reached out towards Sid, but didn't try to grab him. The someone held bulky plastic glasses in her hand. The someone was Elena—the ultimate Cubs fan rooting for the underdog one more time. Suddenly, things didn't feel so empty and fucked any more.

*Author's Note:*
*On June 14, 1991 Marshall Ledbetter held the Florida state capitol building hostage. In his list of demands for releasing the building, he asked for pizza, beer, donuts, and to speak with Jello Biafra, Ice Cube, and Timothy Leary. He was arrested and sent to the Florida State Hospital in Chattahoochee, from which he escaped two months later. This short piece of fiction is dedicated to him.*

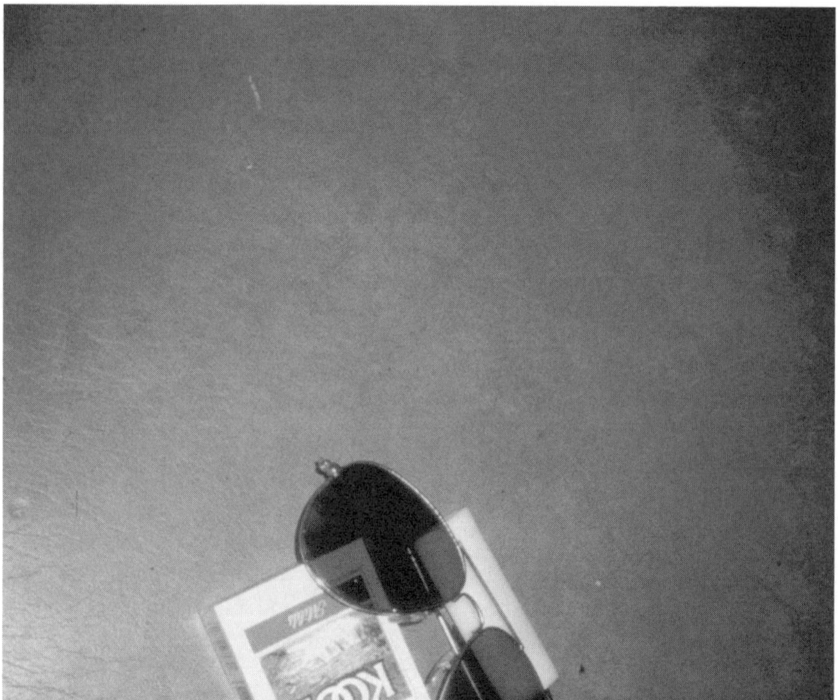
KOOL

# PUNCH AND PIE CONTRIBUTORS

**Bradley Williams** is the creator of the short story zine *Throw That Bottle and Let Me Shoot at It*. His writing has appeared in *Chunklet* and *Razorcake*. While not hounding burlesque dancers, he resides under palm trees and harbors dreams of the Mississippi. He can be reached at <tierra_14@hotmail.com>.

**Ayn Imperato** is a San Francisco writer and musician. She is the author of *Dirty Money* (Manic-D Press) and her writing has appeared in *Razorcake*, *Maximum Rocknroll*, and *Punk Planet*.

**Todd Taylor** is the co-founder of *Razorcake Magazine*. He is very clumsy and has bled from the head while wearing a helmet. He can take the abuse, yet is probably one concussion away from activating some sort of long term insurance. His stuff has been published in *Suburban Voice*, *Thrasher*, *Sassy*, and *Flipside*. He can be reached at: <retodded@razorcake.com>.

**James Jay** lives in Flagstaff, Arizona where he seasonally alternates working as a wildland firefighter and a bartender. He received an MA in English/Literature from Northern Arizona University and an MFA in Creative Writing from the University of Montana. His work has appeared in *Cutbank*, *Thin Air*, *Flipside*, *Big Dan Nielsen's Nerve Bundle Review*, and numerous other journals, and has received two Arizona Commission on the Arts grants. He is the author of *The Undercards* (Gorsky Press 2003).

**Felizon Vidad** was born in the Philippines and grew up on the North Shore of Oahu. She earned her degrees in creative writing at the University of Redlands and Northern Arizona University. Consequently, to pay off those six years of student loans and to support her obsessive serial collecting habits, Felizon taught middle school, high school, and college students in Brevard County, Florida. Currently, she resides in Los Angeles with her husband Sean in an apartment that is a harem of dolls and toys. She welcomes any and all donations and contributions to the Felizon Vidad Doll and Toy Collection.

**Seth Swaaley** is 26 and currently lives in Baltimore. He's spent much of the past five years moving around and working odd jobs. At the time of this printing he was at his twenty-fourth job: parking cars at a children's hospital. The only thing he's had published was a short story in *Razorcake*. He can be contacted at 1211 N. Calvert St. #8, Baltimore, MD 21202.

**Jerry Gabriel** lives in Ithaca, New York, where he's a lecturer in Cornell University's Engineering Communications Program. His stories have appeared in *Fiction*, *Cottonwood*, and *One Story*.

**Jim Munroe** was managing editor at *Adbusters* before writing the novels *Flyboy Action Figure Comes with Gasmask*, *Angry Young Spaceman*, and *Everyone in Silico*. He runs the indie publishing resource site nomediakings.org from his home in Toronto.

**Madeleine Baran** is the creator of the zine *Tight Pants*. Her writing has appeared in *Maximum Rocknroll*, *Razorcake*, *Clamor* and just about every other zine known to man. She currently spends most of her time eating too much cereal and learning more than she ever wanted to know about French people. She can be reached at: <cerealcore@hotmail.com>.

**Wred Fright** has been writing and publishing zines for over a decade now. He is currently publishing a serialized novel in zine form about a garage rock band called *The Pornographic Flabbergasted Emus*, writing stories about Astronaut Urine Gorilla for Fightin' Fun Comics, hacking out a weekly column on zine history for *Babel Magazine*, and singing a song, "A Kiss, A Cheek," on the new vinyl compilation on Cock Punch Records entitled *Let's Get Killed*. He can be reached via email at <wredfright@yahoo.com> and via postal mail at P.O. Box 770332, Lakewood, OH 44107 USA.

**Jim Ruland** would like to thank Scott Southwick, editor of *Fictionline*, for initially publishing "A Terrible Thing in a Place like This." For more information about the events that inspired this counterfactualist account of the Haymarket Affair, check out "Chicago: City of the Century" at <www.pbs.org>. You can follow the links to short profiles of the Chicago Anarchists and enjoy the unintentional comedy of seeing "Self-Publishing" listed under "Tools of Anarchy."

**Patricia Geary** teaches at the University of Redlands and is the author of three highly acclaimed novels, *Living in Ether*, *Strange Toys*, and

*The Other Canyon*. She also practices yoga in Redlands, California, where she lives with her husband, Jack, and son, Denis. *Strange Toys* is the winner of the 1987 Philip K. Dick Award. *The Other Canyon* is available from Gorsky Press.

**Justin Bryant** was born in 1966 in Melbourne, Florida. He has published stories in *The Iconoclast*, *Thin Air*, *The Chiron Review*, *Snowbound*, and *Talk Story*. He graduated from Elon University with a B.A. in English in 2001. He is currently the women's assistant soccer coach at Elon.

**Travis Fristoe** works in a library, typically reads more than he writes, and bikes to the post office most days of the week. Contact: PO Box 13077, Gainesville, FL 32604-1077 or <obscurist@hotmail.com>.

**Sean Carswell** is one of the co-founders and editors of both *Razorcake* magazine and Gorsky Press. His fiction and poetry has appeared in several literary journals over the past ten years. He also has been a staff writer for *Flipside* and *Ink 19*. He is a regular contributor to *Clamor Magazine*, and he has a bi-monthly column in *Razorcake*. He can be reached at: <sean@razorcake.com>.

**Dan Monick** is a freelance photographer based out of Los Angeles. You may not have heard of him before, but if you've picked up an independent hip hop or punk rock magazine in the past few years, or even if you've read your city's weekly newspaper, chances are, you've come across a photo by Dan. To see more of his photos or to contact him, visit: <www.dmonick.com>.

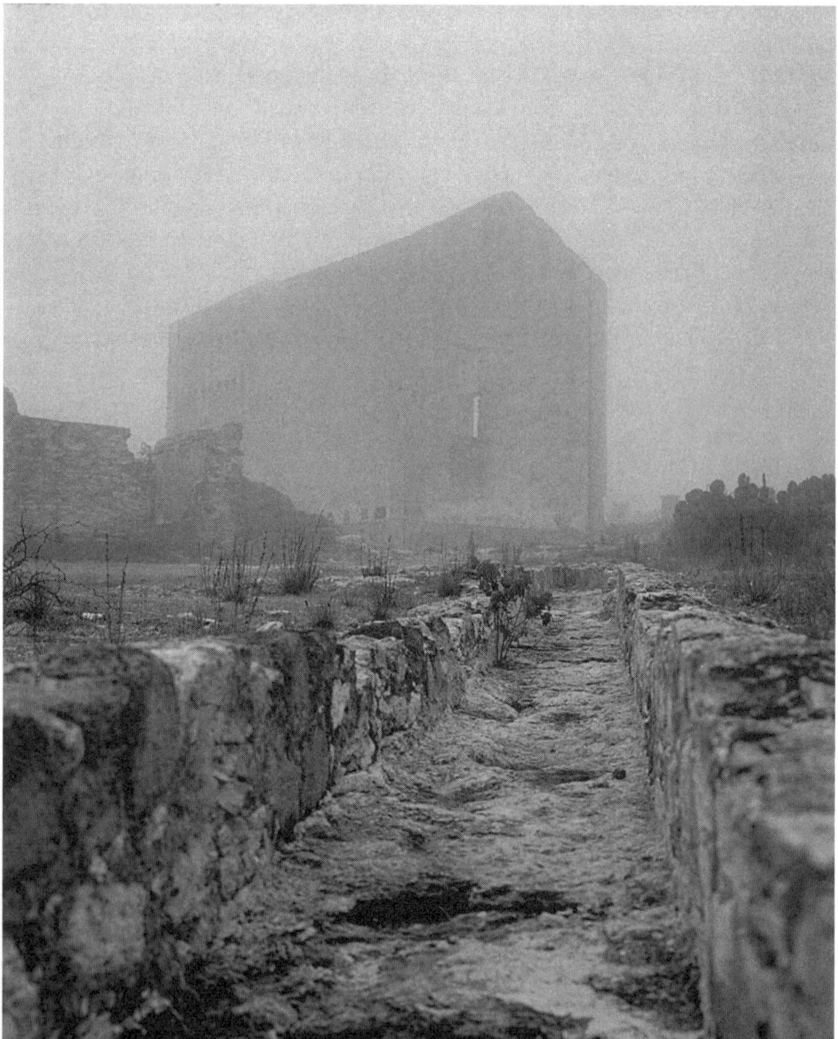